THE UNEXPECTED

To

Tanya

From Author Helen
Collier

read and learn about
a different America

Helen

Helen Collier with Meow at the Helm

i

Life Chronicles Publishing
Give your life a voice!

lifechroniclespublishing.com
ISBN-13: 978-1-950649-05-1
Illustrator: Shakeyna Sterling
Cover Design: Life Chronicles Publishing
Editor: Jada Berteaux
Consultant: John Huguley
Copyright © 2019

TABLE OF CONTENTS

Acknowledgement

Prologue

Page

ACKNOWLEDGEMENT

This work of fiction has been written to acknowledge certain women. Those women looked beyond their privileged place in life to expose the wrongs done to others who had no privileges or human rights. Many gave their time, effort and, sometimes, even their lives to expose those wrongs. The protagonist in *The Unexpected* is one such woman. Dawn's life suddenly changes when she steps out of her privileged world and allows Meow, the Louisiana catfish, to take her back in time to learn a different American history. This is written in tribute to Viola Liuzzo, Anne Brown Adams, Susan Seykato-Smith, Dale Golden, Deborah Jordan, Julie Van Buren, and Anne Guerry Hodderson.

Thanks go out to my mother, Susie Pearl Adams Green, and my twin brother, Eugene Green, for sending their vibrations into my heart to bring forth my message to this earth world. The magic of your lives still flows through me.

Many thanks to my sister, Elsie Mister, retired Director of Nurses, who gave me insight into the world of the unknown.

Much love goes out to my sister, Lavonda Dorsey, who moved things around in her home to give me writing space.

Thank you so much, Sharon Wilson, retired school teacher, who read and supported me on this subject matter.

The Renton Writers Workshop has been the best ever in hours spent giving their editorial advice and research support to this project. Thank you fellow-writers.

The African American Writers Alliance of Seattle, Washington has been a valuable support for me as a Sci-Fiction Writer as well as the North American Writers Association.

Thanks, and love goes out to my children, Susie, Shenee, Weslynn, Mylo and my husband, John. They have always been there for me in support of my writings.

Most of all thanks to the old, black women in the states of Louisiana, Mississippi, Missouri, and Illinois who shared their knowledge of how it was back in the time when slavery, then Jim Crow was a way of life for their grandmothers and great grandmothers. Quietly, I listened to their nightly whispers in the wintertime under the quilting horses and in the summer while the lightning bugs flashed their lights around the smoke from the fires that kept the bugs away. I must acknowledge Harriett Beecher Stowe's main character, a male slave named Uncle Tom, who gave his life to save the lives of two female slaves. A Christian man who, undeservingly, was misrepresented in history.

This Book is dedicated to the spirits of Susie Pearl Adams Green, Pearlie Mae Green Williams, Associate Professor Jane C. Pennell, Frances Campbell, Rosemary Campbell, Margaret Campbell Wiggins, El Marie Mosley, Lucille, Brown Perkins and Grace Cole who left their vibrations with me as they moved into the next stage of life.

PROLOGUE

Nightmares ravaged Dawn's dreams. She stood out in the cotton field; the heat of the sun beamed down on her face. Looking around, she wondered where everyone had gone. Her arms had begun to tan, causing her halter to deflect her skin. The blue shorts she wore hugged her white legs that had also begun to darken. Troughs, like those May Bee and the other female slaves were forced to lie in, stood scattered all around in the cotton field. Dawn saw so many she thought of them as coffins.

The scene scared her when she turned and saw naked white and black men running towards her. Dawn began to run, her heart pounding. Looking to see how close they were upon her; she tripped and fell into one of the troughs. The naked men crowded around her as hot blood rushed to her face. She struggled to keep from being smothered to death. Just as she was about to take her last breath the dream changed, and Dawn found herself standing beside May Bee and her babies at the river bank.

They waited for Meow to come for her. She looked up and down the river, anxious for the catfish's arrival. Dawn wanted to get back to her own century before she found herself in another one of those awful troughs. This was not her century and she didn't want to become a part of it or its horrors.

The sound of dogs barking caused the two women to stare at each other in terror.

"Slave hunters come brang dogs to git May Bee and hur babies." May Bee screamed as she took off running. Down the river bank, May Bee ran with Dawn beside her. Through weeds and over sticks, they ran as sharp brush cut into May Bee's legs drawing blood. Dawn felt the pain of the sharp brush that cut into May Bee's legs, but she kept running. The faster she ran the louder the snarls of the hounds grew. The babies cried as May Bee and Dawn leaped over two large logs in their path. Neither woman stopped until the thick lips and vicious teeth of the hounds had them cornered.

The hounds pulled against their leashes. Saliva poured from their jowls as the red hair on their backs gleamed wet with sweat. There the mistress stood, holding the leashes of her three blood hounds in one hand, her cattail whip in the other. She, like the hounds, breathed deeply as though exhausted by the chase.

"I got your ass now wench. My hounds will eat you for dinner." A satanic glare marred her features as she let the hounds loose on May Bee. Her babies in her arms, May

Bee turned and jumped free-falling into the river. Dawn jumped in behind her as she screamed for Meow to come save her. When she came up for air, May Bee and her babies had disappeared under the water.

CHAPTER ONE
DAWN MEETS MEOW

Dawn sat eating a quiet dinner with her parents. The silence ended when her mother asked how her classes were coming along. She took a deep breath and laid her fork beside her plate.

"I'm twenty-one years old, seated in a college classroom with angry black students who believe this country has screwed up their lives. They seem bitter, for reasons I can't understand. They act as though we owe them something."

Removing his glasses, her father ran his hand through his dark brunette hair as he gazed at her asking,

"What class is this?"

"History, Dad."

"Your interest is in law, isn't it?"

"Yes, but I needed an additional class to finish my electives."

"Good, don't worry about the thoughts of those students. Their life is theirs and yours is yours. You can't understand them any more than they can understand you."

She heard him sigh. "There were three other classes you could have taken but you chose this one. You'll finish soon and have no reason to see those students again. Am I right?"

She smiled at her father in agreement.

"Your mother and I will be going to Canada for a week. Want to come along?"

This meant she would have the house to herself, Dawn thought. It would be good since she had to work on her written and oral report due the following week.

"Dad I would love to, but you know I have school."

"What is it about these students that has you so distraught?" Her mother asked.

Dawn looked at her. Her father often said she was a younger version of her mother. She had to admit, they did look alike except her mother wore her hair short, while her blonde hair flowed down her back.

It wasn't enough for her mother that it was *only one class* as her father had stated; one she would be finished within two weeks and would never have to engage those students again. Her mother always wanted details. It was a requirement for many of their conversations. She knew her mother's words of wisdom had saved her from many disasters when *so-called* friends decided to experiment on the wild side.

Her first year in college she and a girlfriend decided to experiment with a street drug. She came to in the hospital staring blankly at her parents remembering the weird scenes that had surged through her mind. The strange visions were so terrifying she had run out into the street screaming.

Though softly spoken, her mother's voice felt like needles piercing her brain as she said, "You must remember, dear daughter you are not a male who can take chances with his life. The world will most likely forgive his sins. He may commit others that will, no doubt, be forgiven. I'm afraid, my dear, there is little forgiveness for the female. Once her life is soiled with shame, she is doomed to live that shame with no redemption." Her heart wept for the shame she had brought on her parents.

"Those who bring your shame before the public's eyes seeking justice are simply calling attention to it and the shame that marks your life forever. You are responsible for the life God has given you— no one else. Do you understand me?"

"Yes, Mom, I understand."

Now, if anyone suggested taking drugs to Dawn, she turned and went the other way. The shame of one ill-fated experience was enough. She knew she could ill-afford another. Her thoughts on her mother's question, she wondered what words of wisdom she would give her for her newest concern.

"I don't like that those African American students in class speak so negatively about our country. They're always complaining about how American history books have been altered. And, they constantly bring up the subject of Jim Crow, slavery, and the *discrepancy* in the history texts dealings with race relationships in this country. Everyone has, at one time, had a hard time, Mom. Yet, these students always imply that the history books we are studying tell a lukewarm story of black American history while glorifying white American history."

"Everyone has a right to their opinion, dear."

Her mother's statement prompted her to make her point.

"Tony, a black student, screamed out in class, 'Where is God when you need Him? You need a time machine to take you back in history to see how life was for the female slave in this country.' Our debate got so heated our classmates challenged us to give an oral report on the female slave in the eighteenth century. The instructor approved it. If there was any way for me to go back and see for myself how life really was for the female slaves, I could give their life stories the justice they deserve. I don't need to *be* a slave to see what life was like back then. Every American's life is described in history books with nothing left out. I believe even slaves preferred America to the jungles of Africa, Mom!"

"Dawn, my dear, how many black students whose history stems from American slavery do you know personally?"

"I don't have to know them personally," Dawn replied. "It seems strange to me that there are people who live in the same country as I do yet think so differently about it. These people believe this country has wronged them. People I didn't know existed before this class brought me into conflict with them."

Dawn and her mother stared at each other.

"They are bitter for reasons I can't understand."

"Dawn, our ancestors and theirs had a harsh relationship during and after slavery. It is a subject your father and I never discussed with you because we never thought it would be of any concern to you. I suggest you give this oral report some serious thought. Speaking before an audience of angry students will probably bring you grief and further distance you from them."

"I have already agreed to do the report. I can't back out now. As far as distancing myself from them, I've never had a close relationship with any black person."

"Have it your way. It's only a suggestion I hope you will consider." Dawn rose and dropped her napkin on the table, "Have a fun trip. I have lots of studying to do while you two are away."

***

Soon after her parents left that Sunday afternoon, Dawn took off in her gray Mini Cooper. The car was a gift from her parents for her twenty-first birthday. It wasn't a car she would have chosen for herself, but her parents were pleased with their gift. As soon as she finished law school and became gainfully employed, she'd be sporting a Mustang, a car more to her liking.

She parked the Cooper in a tranquil area where the Corps of Engineers had installed an underground gate in a part of the Connecticut River that trapped marine life inside until it was opened. She called it her private sanctuary. It wasn't a park, but it was a nice place to come when she wanted to reflect on concerns. The area was professionally landscaped, and she liked its quiet privacy.

Dawn walked out on the spacious grounds few people visited. Grass covered the landscape. Flowers bloomed in rockeries up the hill and billowing white clouds reflected on the water. Hills melted into the distance. Fresh greenery gave life to what once had been barren land. Summer was in full promise.

Dawn watched, hoping she could spot the huge blue catfish that often cruised along the edge of the water seeming to be searching for a way out. She spied it about a month before as she gazed down into the water looking for signs of fish life. The fish looked to be seven feet long. When she first saw it, she feared it was a shark. It soon occurred to her that the water was fresh, so she knew she was wrong about the species. Dawn had been intrigued by its huge and awesome blue back. For the last three weekends, she had come to watch it move through the water.

It became a secret friend she didn't have to share with anyone. She had been intrigued also by its strange twists and turns. Dawn had never seen a fish that color or with eyes that large. They rolled around its head like giant lime green balls. When the fish swam close to the bank she sat on the grass and complained to it about her problems, which happened to be the three black students in her classroom.

Gazing into the water, she hoped it was still on the inside of the gate. Dawn wondered how it had gotten trapped inside in the first place. She assumed the gate must have closed before it had a chance to swim out. Sometimes the loud noise made by its tail and the water it splashed upon the bank let her know of its discontent.

Dawn steadied her gaze as she looked for it. There was something odd about that fish. It swam around staring up at her as if it had something to say.

What if it really understands what I share with it? She wondered jokingly.

Dawn wondered had it escaped. She stooped down near the edge of the bank and tossed a rock into the water hoping the fish would appear. All at once a huge wave came up and slashed up on shore. Dawn rushed backward, but not fast enough. The wave washed over the bank almost drowning her before she could rescue herself. Drenched by the water, she lay soaked from the downpour.

She quickly wiped her eyes and face so that she could see. The catfish she had been talking to for weeks lay beside her. Its huge blue body wiggled on the bank. The water that flowed from its mouth covered her, as she gasped for air. Her heart raced. It moved around like a big fat pig. Its long whiskers danced on the ground. A wide smile spread across its huge lips. Dawn wanted to run but she couldn't get up.

"*Hello, honey chile sho' glad ya come back to see 'bout ol' Meow.*" Dawn's lips dropped as her mouth flew open.

"*All ya' gotta do is open dat gate and Meow will take ya back down south to two hundred yeers ago.*"

A fish that talks? Oh, my God!

Had she drowned? Dawn stared too stunned to speak. Her entire body trembled as she dug her feet into the soft muddy bank. The fish appeared to be searching for something. Its foot-long whiskers made Dawn nervous as they danced around. Perhaps she had nothing to fear, yet seated there staring at the fish beside her, she didn't know what to do.

"*Don't set thare galkin' at me like we bof' crazy. I been stuck in dis poll'ted water since my cur'osity got de best of me and my friends lef' me behind when thay seed I was doomed. Tol' me to come on out but I was busy lookin' around fo' somethin' interestin' to get ta' when dat gate shut and I got locked inside. "Nother seben days 'for dose fools open dis gate agin, by dat time I wants to be down south long de Lou'siana, Mis'sippi border havin' fun. I needs to git back on home to see 'bout my friends and family down thare waitin' on me."*

Dawn fell backward as the catfish's voice aroused in her a sense of fear. Its eyes fastened on her. She sat beside it with her mouth open staring in shock at the talking fish. Her heart raced as she remembered the trip the drug had taken her on. She hadn't drowned so she must have unknowingly ingested something, but when? And what?

"Come on now, I've been listenin' to yer take on dat American History class and dose black students since ya been comin' out hare. Git dis gate up for Meow so I can take ya back into de world of de slave woman. Ya'll fo sho' write a report dat class can't come close to, eben da black dude ya feel don't got his facts right. All ya gotta do is pull dat red handle down." A smile flashed across the catfish's big, wide, blue face as it stared at Dawn who finally managed to stand up. Her sense of what was real had been shaken and she was desperate to bring herself back to reality.

Dawn looked over at the large lock under the red handle. There was no way she could open it. What were the risks if she dared do what this fish suggested? Something she knew must be impossible. Her eyes stayed glued on the fish hopeful it would disappear.

Was her mind playing tricks on her? She looked down at her wet clothes, then at the fish wondering, not if, but *when* she should start running.

After her first encounter, she had never again dared to experiment with any mind-altering drugs. This seemed too surreal. Maybe, she thought, she was having a flashback. For now, she felt forced to play along with this trick of her mind.

She didn't believe any of this was really happening, or that the fish could do any of the things it said it could do, but she had no choice but to see how this hallucinogenic experience would play itself out. Dawn glanced around to see if there was anyone else nearby only to discover she and the catfish were alone. She moved towards the stairway reaching over the rail to grab the red locked latch that the fish said would free it.

"When will we be going?" she asked with her hands on the red handle.

The catfish wiggled around towards Dawn. Its big lime green eyes rolled around in its head.

"Soon as dat gate opens, we'll be on our way."

This fish was talking to her about going somewhere when Dawn's thoughts were how to get away from it.

"When will we return?" Dawn asked. "After all, I don't want to remain living two centuries ago for very long." She realized she must play along with this surreal scene until her mind somehow returned to normal.

"How long ya thank it will take for ya to git de needed information for dat report?"

"You said the gate won't be open for another week. I'll need at least a week. Then you must bring me back so that I can close the gate before anyone knows it has been opened and have time to write my report and make it to class on time." Dawn laughed to herself wondering when and how this illusion would end.

"Thare's honor in de South ya don't find in many places in dis country 'f ours. We may haf' us some misplaced values but on our honor, ya can cert'ly count. I kin get ya back hare and be gone 'for thay know dat gate's been opened. On my honor as a Lou'siana catfish, I will cert'ly return ya back by den. Is it a deal?"

Dawn looked down at the wet pink halter and blue shorts she wore. "I don't have a change of clothes," she said as she wondered when this eerie scene would end.

"Chile, I been wearing dese same clothes all my life. Don't bother me a'tall. Ya gonna view life in another time not yer own. Only one slave woman, who don't got but one

12

change of clothes hursel, and hur two babies will know ya're thare. Ya won't need a thang just room to fill yer brain with all dat ya gonna learn. I guarn'tee ya, honey chile, thare won't be another report close to de one ya gonna give b'lieve ya me!"

"What slave woman is that?" Dawn asked as she placed her hand on the handle and pressed down on it thinking that the lock would prevent the red handle from opening the gate. The scene would then disappear, and she could hurry home. She didn't even care if she got a ticket as long as she got away from there. She wouldn't be returning again—that's for sure.

The moment she pressed down on the handle the lock opened as the handle released the latch. The gate rose and with her next breath, Dawn found herself swept inside the belly of the catfish. Going, only God knew where.

CHAPTER TWO

MAY BEE

Her head wrapped with a white rag May Bee sat under the big tree she shared her thoughts with on Sundays when she was allowed a little time to herself. The green sack dress she wore lay open exposing her breasts to the nursing babies she held. May Bee gazed across the long river next to the tree. She didn't know what kind of tree it was or the name of the river that seemed to go on forever. What she did know was that the tree had been there longer than she had been living and so had the river. It occurred to her that they had been there longer than all of the slaves who lived on the master's plantation.

The tree was her friend. The only friend she had if the truth be told. She came to sit under it because she felt she needed to clear her thoughts. She could tell it anything and never had to worry about it getting back to the wrong person. It was Sunday, the day the master allowed his slaves their time with the slave preacher he trusted to teach them about

God. Today, May Bee was spending her own time with God seated against her friend.

She scolded herself for letting her babies get too close to her heart.

Knowing, like the others, they would be gone when those who owned her felt like selling them. That week, the mistress had her social visit with her lady friends. An old male slave who served without inappropriate words or actions brought her guests to the plantation. Any inkling of impropriety by the old slave would have promptly been reported by the ladies who would have then casually stood by to watch his body swing from the nearest tree.

May Bee watched her mistress's guests hurry into her parlor as they chattered among themselves while she listened to their conversation. Not that they cared if May Bee heard, they believed those they enslaved lived without a bit of sense, not understanding that they were being talked about. May Bee poured wine for them in the wine glasses the mistress never allowed the slaves to touch except to wash or serve. The shorter female guest picked up her wine-filled glass, "I see that husband of hers has been playing in the dirt again."

May Bee watched her mistress's guests chuckle and peep out the door to make sure their conversation wasn't overheard by the mistress.

"I saw as well," the taller female guest said also sipping her wine.

As soon as she entered the room, May Bee's mistress sent May Bee to clean in the next room. She hurried out but not before she watched the three women warmly embrace. From the next room, she could hear the taller guest say, "We must get a handle on these wenches and those messes they are having. Saw two of them holding their messes when we were driven in." "White as one of us, I dare say." May Bee peeped into the room and saw the shorter guest eye the other who stood grinning.

"My husband says he can't get away from them. They are after him all the time, poor soul," the mistress stated in defense of her husband.

May Bee knew her mistress sat fanning herself at that very moment. She always fanned herself when she had fixed up some lie. Any fool, May Bee thought to herself, would have to know better. Even she, as dumb as the mistress insisted she was, knew better of the lie being told on her and the other slave women.

Mammie, an old female slave, had taken May Bee under her care when she was brought there after being sold away from her mother. While tending her needs, Mammie told her how it would be soon as she was old enough to carry water, which was nine or ten. The old woman, she learned, had lived on different plantations having been bought and sold many times for taking her babies and running off to keep them from being sold away from her.

"We makes de babies de massa got to work the fields and tend his mistress and clean thay house. De men most in the field, us work in de field and in de house." May Bee listened not really understanding what the old woman was telling her until several years later when two of the water pails she carried turned into the master's babies. Many who worked the fields were his children; slaves much lighter than the ones he bought.

"We clean thay houses and take care of thay women folk," the old woman told her. "Thay babies dat come from thay women folk is always fed our milk 'fore ours. If thay 'llow ours to live for a while wit us and not be sold away so dat all de milk we give go to thay babies. Adder de baby come, massa come lay with us agin."

May Bee soon understood, by *lay,* she meant to give their bodies to their masters when they wanted sex. She did

18

not know the word was called sex, but she did know that she had looked down between her legs and told God if she knew what the master was so hot after down there, she would snatch it out. She would then kill it dead so he would go back to his house with his wife and get from her what May Bee didn't want to give him. But there he was most nights waking her to move her babies out of his way.

Her master was an important judge in the state. Why would he want to be on that dirty old sack? She couldn't understand it. She sure hated sleeping on it with her babies, but it was all she had and with no time to clean it, it seemed a part of the dirt the mistress said she was. It was only after she had given birth that her master would find another slave woman to lay with. In a day or so he returned to lay with her again.

May Bee had seen the scornful look on her mistress's face after making her way down to the shack to see who this new baby looked like. It was as white as the judge. The little hair she had was corn yellow just like his and her nose was as pug as the Judge's. This one was his—just like the others. The mistress gave May Bee an evil glare as if *she* had done something wrong.

The master didn't allow any other men to have sex with the slave women without his permission. Not even the overseers dared do so without his blessing. That day she stood listening to the mistress tell her friends that they, the slave women, kept after him. She could tell them the truth, but she knew they didn't want to hear the truth. She now listened to the two guests exclaiming that their husbands and other men in the family had the same problem. *What liars!* May Bee thought to herself.

"Scandalous! I believe the wenches would open their legs to dogs if they could have them," one of her guests stated. "I've told my husband he must be careful. There is something about those loose wenches that makes them less than human."

"Our men are so vulnerable," May Bee heard another voice cackle as she peeped inside the room again to see them all fanning. "It is becoming such that we must get a handle on it and one of the ways is to sell all those babies down the river to whoever will buy the messes." May Bee was stricken by what she heard.

"You're right," she listened to her mistress say. "Thieves, the lot of them. Caught one gal in the kitchen scraping food off the plates me and my husband left. Started to have her whipped but let her go on and feed those messes of hers cause I knew what was coming."

May Bee trembled thinking about the whip the mistress often used to beat her with when she had fed her babies those scraps. They wouldn't be so hungry come evening when she returned with them to her shack. She worked in the fields most of the day then cleaned the mistress's house until supper time finally came. As soon as the babies saw her, they scratched and pulled for something to be put in their mouths like little birds waiting in a nest. She wanted to beg for her children not to be sold this time, but she knew the mistress would have no mercy for babies who looked so much like her husband.

May Bee saw her looking down from her window early some mornings watching her husband leave her shack. She had seen the hate for her seething in the eyes of the mistress.

May Bee pressed her head against her friend the tree. She knew if slave women were seducing the master, their necks would be hanging from that tree. Since the mistress was not allowed to hang anyone, only suggest that it be done, neither she nor the other slaves females would fall to that fate as long as the plantation master's appetite for black bodies lasted. It seemed his addiction was growing more insatiable by the day.

Her mistress had been blessed with only two babies for the master and they both died before birth. She claimed it was caused by his keeping company with the black wenches he needed to rid himself of. Of course, he kept right on visiting the shacks ignoring the advice she so sternly gave. That was years ago when she was a young woman, and the babies she lost meant something to her if not to her husband.

Who I's gonna love when dese babies sol'? May Bee thought.

"Whare is God when you need Him?" she asked herself aloud tossing a rock into the river.

A small ripple flowed across the brown water followed by a larger ripple and then a great wave rose bringing with it a blue catfish bigger than any she had ever seen or heard tell of. From its big wide mouth fell a young white woman. Her long hair as yellow as that of the babies she held. May Bee's mouth dropped wide open as she stared at the woman dressed like no white woman she had ever seen before. She gazed with wide eyes at the woman lying on the ground taking in the air around her. May Bee feared what would happen next. She had never seen anything like it in her life. It had her as mortified as the day she found herself and her mother being carried away in the middle of the ocean on a boat with strange white beings she had never seen before.

She wanted to run back to her shack and the other slaves, but she clung to her babies pressing her back against the tree. The slave woman stared ahead, her eyes bulging as she strained to understand this new and strange phenomena that had come upon her.

The entire journey took only a few seconds. In fact, Dawn's arrival happened so fast she had no time to think about where she was going or what would become of her. Except for the river bank, trees stood over every inch of the earth in this environment. Birds flew overhead as squirrels scrambled to reach higher branches in the trees. Everything seemed almost mystical. Dawn gazed wide-eyed at the landscape around her. She was in a part of the country she had never visited before. The catfish lay in front of her on the bank of the river where it had spit her out. Its tail moved back and forth as its belly moved in and out. It wiggled back into the water with only half its body out.

The sudden sound of babies screaming increased Dawn's fears as she sat up and scanned the thickly wooded area. Staring at a tall tree near the river's edge, she spotted a frail black woman seated against it nursing two white babies.

Dawn's thoughts ran wild as she gazed at the black woman and the white babies suckling her breasts. She'd been swept into the unknown. Where had this catfish taken her?

"Where are we?" she urgently questioned the catfish.

The catfish opened its month and burped out water as it stared from Dawn to the woman and her babies.

"Lou'siana, honey chile."

"Louisiana! What year is this?"

"Why, honey chile, dis is de yeer eighteen hun' and fort-two."

"Eighteen forty-two?" Dawn trembled as she looked again at the woman and the babies in her arms. It suddenly occurred to her that this was a real live slave woman living in bondage. Dawn's iPad was nearly two hundred years away in her car along with her cell phone. A picture of a slave woman with two white babies nursing at her breasts would go viral on social media!

"Ya come to take my babies from me ain't ya? I know'd da mistress go take 'em." May Bee cried out as she pulled the babies closer to her.

That catfish actually kept its word, Dawn thought. *It took me back in time!* Dawn trembled as she stared at the woman and the babies she held. She listened to her speak in a dialect she had never heard before. The hands that held those babies looked rough and leathery.

The woman's dress was open in the front exposing her breasts that looked much too large for her frail body. It wasn't until she gazed into the eyes of the slave woman that she saw in them the fear of what might happen to her and the babies she held.

Dawn looked down at the catfish. *When would she return to her own time? Would she be stuck here for the rest of her life?* She waited hopeful the slave woman would speak again. Meow yawned and spoke instead.

"*May Bee,*" the catfish said moving around toward the woman to give her his full attention. The slave woman stared wide-eyed at the fish that had just spoken her name. She was scared to death and hoped her mistress would not find her out there with this half-naked white woman wearing almost nothing and a big old, blue talking catfish.

"What's dat ya wont wit May Bee?"

"*Dawn done come hare to help ya keep yer babies.*"

Dawn watched May Bee's eyes grow alert but soon saw a smile replace the frown on her face.

"Those are her babies?" Dawn asked. Her eyes widened as she stared at the white looking babies and listened to the catfish talk to the slave woman.

25

"Me babies?" May Bee said as she looked lovingly at her children.

"*Yes, Dawn, dem's hur babies. May Bee dis white woman comes from de future and she knows how to handle ya mistress to keep hur from sellin' yer babies. Nobody'll be able to see hur but ya and yer babies. She'll be wit ya till she helps ya keep yer babies wit nobody knowin' she's wit ya. Ya understan' dis May Bee?*"

"Yuh, suh."

The catfish's announcement of what she was going to do for the slave woman caused Dawn's mouth to stretch wide open. She wondered why a woman as dark as the woman she was looking at would want to keep babies as white as the ones she held.

"Whare's God when ya need 'em? Always somewhares. I sho' thank ya cause thay's all I got to love. I don lost mor 'sides dese hare."

Tears fell from May Bee's eyes as she rubbed the bellies of the nursing babies who had quieted under the comforting hands of their mother.

Dawn gasped thinking it strange to hear Tony's words about God coming from the mouth of this slave woman two centuries before either of them were born. She moved closer to the catfish and whispered, "Meow, why did you tell her I came to help her keep her babies? You know I don't know how to handle the people back in this century. I better hope I don't get sold into slavery myself. They aren't going to listen to me tell them anything dressed like no white woman they've ever seen before." Dawn knew the shorts and halter top she wore weren't appropriate for this adventure—an adventure that had already proven to be much more than she bargained for.

"Ya don't have to worry 'bout tryin' to convin't nobody of anythang cause thay ain't able to see or hare ya. Only May Bee and hur babies will be able to do dat and since dat big baby gurl ain't but 'bout a yeer ol' and the lit' baby gurl ain't but four months at best, neith' one can talk so dat won't be no problem fo' ya."

Dawn looked at the two babies and noticed that the one on the right was much larger than the one on the left. The smaller baby, having lost her mother's nipple, moved her mouth around searching for it.

Dawn heard in her mind the catfish say things to her unheard by the slave woman. *"Now, ya can jes be an observah but if ya reilly wanta top dat black dude's report, ya can be a partic'pant. None 'f what happens to May Bee will actually happen to ya, but I kin make it so's ya feels what May Bee feels. When she be happy or sad ya'll be one or de*

27

otter. When she eat ya eat, when she feel hungry ya' will too. Hur pain will become yer pain."

Thoughts of having a report better than Tony's nearly erased Dawn's fears. After all, Meow reassured her none of what might happen there would actually happen to her. The thrill of having the best report chilled her mind of anything else. "You can do all of that Meow? Really make me feel her emotions?" *Wait until the class hears what I'll have to tell them,* Dawn thought as her fears completely evaporated.

"Dat ain't all I can do. Now hurr' up and tell Meow which one ya want to do, honey chile."

"When and how will I get back to the future, Meow? I hope you don't plan to leave me here for the rest of my life now that you are free. You did give me your word." The catfish looked over at May Bee and her babies.

"May Bee ya mus' brang Dawn back to me de very nex' time de massa 'llows ya to come sit under dis tree. I be waitin' fo' hur right hare. Dat'll be de nex' ol' preacher day ya har?" Dawn looked from the catfish to May Bee, who looked at them both.

"If she gon' help me keep me babies I sho' brang hur back to ya right at dese place when de time comes." May Bee seemed to understand most of their conversation.

"Dawn, May Bee will brang ya back to dis har bank by de river's edge. I be waitin' fer ya right har."

Dawn wondered if the slave woman really understood what the catfish was telling her.

"Well, what's it gon' be, as an observah or feelin' what she feels? Mind ya, none what happin' to May Bee will be happnin' to ya. Ya'll simply 'perience de emotions stirrin' in May Bee's body."

Dawn sighed as she gazed at May Bee. "If it will make my report better than Tony's, I must experience her emotions. After all, I will always be myself with no physical changes, right?"

"No, but a hell 'f a mind change I 'pect." Meow winked and Dawn wondered exactly what that wink meant.

"Meow don't you be late because you have to return me home so I can close that gate and write my report. And don't get to having so much fun you forget to come for me," Dawn added as an afterthought.

"Thare's honor in de south an' I'm from Lou'siana. I will return on time."

"But what if I need to talk to you before that time?"

"Just say Meow and I'll enter yer thoughts an' see what ya see. I won't be able to change a thang; I'll only be able to explain what's goin' on. Cause ya won't be known

29

to dose 'round ya, yer life will be safe but remember on de seventh day ya must be hare by de river's edge."

One quick splash and the catfish was gone.

Dawn gazed into the water. Her heart sank when Meow disappeared. The catfish had left her there. Whether she wanted to be or not, she was no longer in the year 2016 but now lived in the year 1842. She turned and stared at May Bee. She read the slave woman's mind, and felt her trembling.

She sat still holding tight to the babies in her arms. May Bee had just seen Dawn pop out of a fish's mouth, something Dawn knew must have the slave woman terrified. While she didn't feel threatened by May Bee, someone seeing them there together could cause May Bee to be punished, or possibly killed. Dawn was still not sure anyone else could see her.

The slave woman rose from where she sat still gazing at Dawn. Dawn knew she was about to take off. She had better say something quick or she would be left there.

"May Bee. Do you want me to help you keep your babies? I know you love them." She felt the slave woman's emotion of love as she hugged her babies. She looked at Dawn and rubbed the heads of her babies with her chin. Dawn felt May Bee's fear subside.

"Thay's all May Bee got to love. Help me keep 'em 'f ya's can. I sho' 'preciate it." Dawn smiled pulling her hair behind her back.

"We have seven days in which to do it. You must take me back to the plantation where you live so that I can find a way to help you keep them." Dawn stared at May Bee to give assurance she could do what the catfish told the slave woman she could do. Dawn also felt her indecisiveness. The slave woman didn't move. She just stood staring at her. Dawn realized something else was wrong, something she didn't understand. Then it came to her. She saw what May Bee saw. Dressed in those shorts and halter wouldn't be something that she could safely wear in 1842.

"May Bee, no one can see me but you and your babies." Dawn wasn't sure no one could see her or that she would be able to help her keep her babies. She knew however she didn't plan to sit by that river alone for a week waiting for that catfish to return. The slave woman had to be convinced it was safe to take her back to the plantation.

"You be's a ghos' spirit from God come from up yonder?" May Bee looked skyward as she spoke.

Dawn looked up with her. "Yes, May Bee, God sent me to help you keep your babies, but you must take me back with you to make that happen."

Dawn knew it was the only thing that made sense to the slave woman and since she didn't know how she got there herself, it made sense to her, too. May Bee moved away from the tree and started walking barefoot down a weedy path. Dawn felt the hard ground under her shoes as she followed her, glad she had worn her Nikes. The slave woman walked as though she was in a hurry to get where she was going. Dawn trotted behind her trying to keep up. In seven days, she would return from this place back to the modern world unchanged. She hoped.

CHAPTER THREE

DAWN'S AWAKENING

It seemed they would walk forever. Dawn wondered how long it would take to get to the plantation. The light brown eyes of the larger baby gazed back at her as she rode her mother's hip. Dawn knew that since both babies saw her pop out of the catfish's mouth, both would always see her just as their mother would. She kind of wished the babies could talk; they probably could tell her things about their lives that would highlight her oral report.

Dawn reflected on this journey she was about to embark upon. It couldn't be too bad, she reasoned. She had already informed her classmates that everyone who came to this country for the first time had difficulty adjusting. In her heart, she knew nothing in America could possibly be as bad as living in Africa with all its wild animals. Dawn believed this had to be true. She didn't know how God played a part in all of this, but she was thrilled at the knowledge that somehow this strange twist of fate offered her the opportunity to see for herself what life was like for the female slave. Now she would be able to give the best report of what she knew had to be true.

What she planned to do was to cram Tony, Shirley and Tina full of what really happened back then. Dawn wondered how they would counter her report. Her friends always called her Miss Perry Mason because she looked at a subject matter in ways others didn't. Dawn pinched herself to see if she was really walking behind a slave woman. What a strange adventure, one she would never forget. It didn't matter that she couldn't share it with her friends. She didn't need to. Dawn smiled as she followed behind May Bee. She looked at the two babies the slave woman carried, wondering who had fathered them. Dawn decided to engage May Bee in a conversation but had to walk fast to catch up with her.

"Is your real name May Bee, or is that just what they call you?"

"I be May Bee; maybe I is, maybe I ain't." The words came out slow and with caution as May Bee scanned the river to see what else might surface.

They passed an open area and Dawn saw fields of white, fluffy snowballs planted inside green leaves. She knew they had to be cotton as she watched them sway in the summer breeze. Her thoughts turned to how hot it was as she touched her forehead. *It's early spring in Connecticut, it must be midsummer here,* she thought to herself. The unbearable heat smothered her face.

Just when she thought they would never stop walking, they came to a clearing. Dozens of people stood around. The color of the people was the first thing that caught Dawn's attention. Not all the slaves were black skinned as she believed the slaves that came from Africa would be. In fact, most were brown or light to almost white. She looked at the babies May Bee carried, there were many babies that looked like them. She thought about Tony who referred to himself as *Mulatto.*

Some of these people looked as though they had arrived from Europe instead of Africa. Many were as white as she was. All around her, Dawn saw people ill-dressed and undernourished, the same as May Bee and the two babies she carried. None of the babies she saw wore clothing. Only makeshift rags covered their bottoms. The clothing of the older children, also makeshift, hardly covered their bodies.

Before them stood rows of wooden shacks. Dawn started to count them but was distracted by the sound of high-pitched screams. She hid behind May Bee when two women ran up to them and took her babies. Two more pulled May Bee along with them. They seemed not to notice Dawn.

She took a deep breath, happy when she discovered no one could see her. May Bee looked back at her. Dawn smiled and placed her finger up to her lips. She followed close behind May Bee towards the wooden shack where the screams grew louder. She watched other women rush inside. Dawn looked ahead of May Bee to see what all the excitement was about.

Her hand moved up to cover her mouth as she stared in shock. The overpowering smell of fresh blood made her nauseous. It flowed across the floor from the bodies of the women lying there. She had never seen childbirth except on film and never natural childbirth. She now witnessed it. Dawn counted twenty women of different ages about to deliver babies. She looked in shock at the women on the floor screaming with their naked bodies exposed to any viewers who might walk by. Their suffering overwhelmed her as she thought again of her iPad and cell phone. She wanted to kick herself for leaving them.

"My God!" she whispered pressing her lips together. They hadn't been inside ten minutes before two women gave birth right into the hands of May Bee. Dawn knew the health department would have had a field day in this place. With no soap or fresh water, their bloody hands expertly caught each baby.

Women poured green water over the screaming newborns as they came forth. Others cared for the mothers. The sight of three young girls, who couldn't have been more than eleven or twelve laying with their legs spread open waiting to give birth, made Dawn suck air into her lungs as her hands moved to cover her heart. Their bodies convulsed with painful contractions and the fear in their eyes gave witness to the horrors of the birthing conditions.

Dawn wanted to turn and run from the room, but she couldn't leave without May Bee who bent over to deliver another baby. It didn't move or scream when it came out. Dawn shook her head as she watched May Bee place it next to several more who were not breathing. The infant's mother began to cry. The ones who came out alive were given to their mothers. Late into the night, babies came screaming from the bodies of the female slaves lying on the dirt floor.

After the last baby was born, Dawn followed May Bee into another shack to retrieve her babies. When they left, she stumbled behind May Bee in a dazed state of shock.

May Bee took them into a wooded area. The full moon stood as a welcome blessing. Without the benefit of its light, the darkness would have prevented Dawn from seeing anything around her. May Bee sat her babies on the ground then bent down as if to look for something. Dawn watched her quickly pull leaves from a small weed patch and put them in her mouth. She began to chew. Their bitter taste enveloped Dawn's taste buds calming the nausea in her stomach and she remembered the choice she made to experience what the slave woman experienced. Though she couldn't see the weed patch, she wondered what kind of leaves grew on it that not only quieted the nausea in her stomach but also eased the hunger she felt. They headed out of the wooded area.

Soon they entered another shack. May Bee sat the two babies on the floor while she lit an oil lamp. Dawn saw a snake crawl from a large brown sack spread across the floor. She shuddered in fear as May Bee caught and twisted its neck, tossing it outside through an open wall plank. Dawn held her arms together shaking as her eyes searched the shack for more.

No furniture to speak of stood inside the shack except some rags that lay in a pile and the large sack the snake crawled from. A stool sat in a corner. May Bee began to fill the sack with hay and corn shucks. Dawn suddenly realized this was where the slave woman lived. The lumpy sack she filled, Dawn discovered, was May Bee and her babies' bed. May Bee took a seat on the makeshift stool and put more of the leaves into her mouth to chew. She then picked up her babies. The leaves May Bee chewed didn't taste so bitter to

Dawn after a while. The babies rooted for their mother's breasts and the room grew very quiet. With nowhere else to sit she cautiously eased herself onto the dirt floor looking out for more snakes as she watched the babies nurse.

Dawn filled the thick silence with a question, "May Bee, are you a midwife for the women here?"

May Bee stared at her, a puzzled look on her face. Dawn realized she didn't understand what she was asking her. She laid back to spread her legs and placed her hand as if to catch a baby just as May Bee had done for the women giving birth. A smile lit up May Bee's face as she looked from her nursing babies to Dawn.

"May Bee catch dem babies dat come from thare. Me catches 'em. Some neber come har, thay goes right to heben."

Dawn had to say the word to herself several times before she understood what May Bee meant.

"Is heaven a good place for the babies?"

"Dat ol' preacher sez da's a good place. I wonts mines to go thay if thay gotta go from me."

Dawn felt May Bee's sadness gathering inside her.

The room grew quiet again and May Bee laid with her sleeping babies on the sack she had filled.

The lamp slowly burned out. Dawn's eyelids grew heavy and she looked around for a place to sleep. She soon realized there was nowhere to sleep except with May Bee and her babies on the bed of straw and corn shucks. As she lay beside them, Dawn gazed outside the see-through planks hoping another snake wouldn't crawl through. She looked up as billions of stars burned like tea lights against the black blanket of a midnight sky. The bright light of the full moon that filtered into May Bee's home made her more aware of her desolate surroundings. She turned and twisted as she lay uncomfortable on the corn shucks and straw.

By the time Dawn's eyes finally closed, they flew open again. She felt movement next to her. May Bee lifted her babies up from where they slept. Dawn sat up, startled by the large, stocky figure that hovered over them. Fearful of what it meant, she followed May Bee out of her shack into another where she gave her sleeping babies to the women inside.

She and May Bee returned without the babies and May Bee removed her sack dress and spread her naked body across the straw bed. Dawn could not see who the naked person was who straddled May Bee but she screamed as air escaped her lips in a rush from the weight of the large, stocky body suddenly pressing hard against May Bee's body. Dawn felt that they would be smothered to death. The movement in the bed increased and Dawn felt her vagina being sawed in two. Dawn was experiencing what was happening to May Bee. The intruder screamed out as he emptied his sperm inside May Bee. Dawn's body chilled at the sound and feel of his ejaculation. As tears flooded her eyes, Dawn's first thoughts were to call the police and the people in the other shacks to get help but quickly realized this was 1842, not 2016. This *was not rape but* life for the female slave. No matter how wrong she thought it was, there was nothing she could do. Dawn watched the intruder lay back on the bed of straw and rest his arm across May Bee's breasts pinching and squeezing her nipples. Dawn covered her own breasts as she cried and listened.

"Soon, it'll be mating time. I want you to get the rest of them wenches in your row made ready. Have them tell the wenches in the rest of the rows to get ready as well. If they've started to bleed, I want them at the mating party."

Suddenly Dawn understood that this voice belonged to the plantation owner. The multiple births she had just witnessed didn't come from love or the desire of the women to have babies but from the plantation owner's slave mating and labor producing schedule.

"Yuh' suh," she heard May Bee mumble.

"We got about a hundred bucks coming up to mate this season. Maybe I will get fifty or sixty births from you wenches once you are bred. I paid over a hundred dollars to have 'em come in. Course, I got over two hundred for those bucks I took out to mate. Speck I'll have at least a dozen more bucks and wenches in the fields come next season." He grunted then continued, "I'm getting up in age. I need to rest more. Have more 'f yours and the other's runnin' 'round my feet."

Dawn wondered if the females could only have sex when the plantation owner said so. If that was the case, having sex with May Bee gave him the right to determine when and if she had babies.

Where are the babies by his wife? They are the ones that should be running around his feet, Dawn thought as she listened to the one-sided conversation.

"Bought that land next to mine. The price of cotton has gone up now. It's time to expand and get more wenches mated so's I can have workers in the coming seasons."

Dawn listened as her mind traveled back to those poor women's bodies he was using to make himself rich.

"Got me some new slaves from across that ocean. Had them put in the pit 'til they're broken in and understand what they're being told to do. May Bee, make sure no shoes are given them. I can't have them running off— especially during cotton picking season."

"Yuh'suh."

Dawn thought to herself, *there he goes again telling his slave what his plans are. He should be having that conversation with his wife.* She wondered what his wife was like and why he wasn't in bed with her.

Up on his elbow, Dawn felt him squeeze May Bee's breasts again then lay his hairy beard next to them. Soon he rose, dressed and left.

"Oh, May Bee," Dawn whispered when they returned with her babies. "That was awful."

"Massa ain't so bad. Dem big bucks dat ya gotta tussl' wit—dat's a mess!"

Dawn lay there stunned at her reply. What big bucks was she speaking of? How could they be worse than what she had just felt? It occurred to Dawn that May Bee had no idea of the crime committed against her body. Could the bucks be any worse than what she had already witnessed? If so, how would she be able to survive the next six days?

Dawn thought about Tony and the report he must be planning. He typically sat with his legs crossed waiting for her arrival. He had challenged Dawn's ability to research and report the truth about female slavery in America. Only

Dawn and Tony would give competing oral reports in front of the class.

She knew the rest of the class waited anxiously to see which report would be most truthful. Since it was the history of the women of Tony's race, Dawn knew everyone believed it would be impossible for her report to be as accurate as his.

CHAPTER FOUR

DAY ONE

Dawn had not risen from bed before twelve o'clock since high school. Now, here she was twenty-one years old in the year 1842 half asleep seated on a corn shuck mat before the break of day. It was Monday morning, her first full day with the slave woman called May Bee. Dawn yawned as she peered through the cracks between the planks.

"May Bee, it's still dark outside. Where are you taking me this early in the morning?"

"To da cott' fiel,' gotta git me babies put 'fo we go."

Still exhausted from the events of the night before, Dawn made no attempt to rise. She watched May Bee reach beside the stool and dip her fingers into a small can. From it, she rubbed a greasy substance over her body and that of her two babies making them all smell like vanilla. Dawn yawned again wondering what was in the greasy substance that gave it that smell.

As hot as it already was that early in the morning, she watched May Bee wrap a thick rag around her neck and

45

back. Her babies in her arms, she stood and stared down at Dawn. They looked at each other and Dawn scanned the small shack remembering the snake whose neck May Bee had wrenched the night before. She jumped up and beat May Bee and her babies outside.

Dawn followed May Bee into one of the shacks where she dropped off her babies to three older women. They hurried to catch up with the others walking in the dark. Along the way, they all stopped and picked up large sacks. Dawn wondered what they were for. Soon she saw the rows of snowballs glistening in the dark. She remembered them from the day before and realized they were at the cotton fields.

May Bee and the other slaves started their cotton picking. Dawn heard horse hoofs as the slaves placed cotton into the large sacks they carried. It seemed like an hour later before daylight broke. She spied several White men on horseback riding through the rows, whips in their hands and guns strapped to their waists.

By mid-morning the sun was so hot Dawn thought she would faint. May Bee and the others continued to separate the cotton from the leaves and put them into their sacks. She noticed they never looked up at the men on horseback. Some of the slaves had large blisters on their necks and backs. She now understood why May Bee wore that long- sleeved dress and wrapped thick cloth around her neck and back.

The only break allowed the slaves by the riders was to drink a few paltry sips of water from the dipper in the pails carried by enslaved children. The green water was warm and looked unclean. Dawn shook her head in disgust as she stared at the men on horseback—the plantation overseers— drank clear looking water from glass bottles. They moved back and forth throughout the crowd of slaves who picked cotton like they were machines. She saw no concern for them in the eyes of the men who took delight in snapping their whips back and forth in the air.

Dawn watched in horror as two overseers drew back their whips and lashed out at a slave after a young blonde wide chested, white man shouted that the slave was working too slowly. The slave, whose back was already covered with blisters, fell to the ground. The overseer threatened to whip him again as he struggled but failed to get up. Several slaves were directed to throw him into a ditch despite his pleas and quivering body—signs that he was still alive.

The work continued with no further thought of him. Transfixed by the horror, Dawn stared from the slaves to the overseers. Her senses unraveling until the sound of a baby crying drew Dawn's attention to one of the women behind her. The young woman had just given birth the night before. She remembered her because her baby was born as white as May Bee's babies.

How horrible, Dawn thought, *that the girl should be resting.* The young, blonde haired, wide-chested overseer who had the slave thrown into the ditch looked over as the infant's cries grew louder. In the mother's attempt to quiet the baby before it was discovered, Dawn watched as the infant fell from the mother's apron down between two rows of cotton.

The overseer rode up, looked down at the screaming baby then carefully placed the foot of his horse over the tiny infant trampling it until nothing was left but a puddle of blood and skin. Dawn stood paralyzed. It was as if she had been swept into a diabolic horror film. No one looked up or down as the mother wept silently for her murdered child.

"Git back to work fore ya ass is down thare, too!" Dawn sensed from May Bee that the heartless overseer was the father of the baby he had just killed. Slowly the young girl began again to pick cotton. The others, including May Bee, picked as though nothing of interest had just occurred.

"You son of a bitch!" Dawn screamed. On an impulse, she picked up a stick and beat the overseer while calling out to the catfish that had brought her there, "Meow come help me!"

"My Lord, gurl he can't see ya or feel de stick ya beatin' him wit."

"Meow get me out of here. Now! This is too much. He stomped a newborn baby to death. His own baby! The fool had a man thrown into a ditch while still alive! If there's worse, I don't want to see it."

"Dawn dis happened over two hunder'd yeers ago. Yer 'turnin' back home ain't gon' make a bit 'f difference in dat baby's def or thousands more like it dat died da same way."

"A thousand more? That's too barbaric!"

"Dis Lou'siana, honey chile. What ya 'pect? Be thankful I didn't drop ya off in Geo'gia or Miss'ippi. And frien' may I remind ya dat thare's southern states with hunders of plantations whare de horrors of slave life is worse. Some thangs I peeped out 'f dat river wouda made ya crawl back to yer momma's womb."

Dawn continued to cry.

"Anyhow, didn't I promise ya dat yer report would be like no otters in yer class, and I do mean no otters. Now ya won't be able to write in yer report dat white men trampled slave babies to death. De shock of dat news would

stun yer classmates an' dat 'structah who don't know a hill'f beans but what he don' read in books. Thay'd all insis' ya're lyin.' Ya sho'can write dat slaves thrown out to die in de sun won't no crime. Dat'll be enough to start thay blood a pumpin.' Thank about it, if Meow hadn't dumped ya off into May Bee's world, no histry book wouda gave ya dat info'mation. Thay wonts to b'lieve dat it too savage fo' civ'lized folk to have done back den."

"This is too much for me, Meow. I'm ready to return. Right now!" Dawn screamed.

Ya got six more days to go. Don't ya give up now. I was down on the Lou'siana border wit' some friends of mine I hadn't seen in a while. 'Member now, May Bee had to live with hur bondage forty-seven yeers of hur life, showly a worldly morten day gurl like yerself can last another six days. Thare's much more to learn if yer report is gonna mean somethin.' I'm on my way to the Ten'ssee River— got friends waitin' on me."

The voice no longer with her, Dawn walked around in a daze unable to rid herself of the sick feeling that had developed in her stomach. It was worse than her feelings about the birth ritual that already rocked her world.

"May Bee, he killed that newborn baby."

May Bee never stopped picking cotton as she whispered, "Gurl, ya go git yurself kilt whippin on dat white massa."

"He couldn't see me or feel the licks, May Bee."

"Thanks God for dat," May Bee said as Dawn felt her trembling.

"May Bee her baby was murdered."

"Lese wise she in heben now." Dawn stared at the slave woman's back as she put another cotton ball in her sack. She could not believe she thought good had come from the infant's death.

"He needs his ass stomped to death, May Bee, just like he stomped that helpless baby to death."

Before May Bee could answer, a wagon drove up and stopped in front of them. A male slave sat in the wagon and waited. May Bee and five other slave women laid their sacks on the ground and climbed aboard. Dawn followed along after them as she watched May Bee and the others wipe sweat from their faces. Dawn wiped her own face feeling the flames of the hot sun lick her burning cheeks. *Where on earth were they going?* Dawn thought. She looked back at the cotton field as they drove off. There were surely enough poor souls left out there slowly burning to death. She was so glad she was no longer one of them.

****

As the wagon took them away, Dawn's thoughts turned to May Bee. The slave woman would live to reach about fifty-four years of age, Dawn estimated as she wondered about May Bee and her strange ways. Worked worse than a man would work an animal, her body carried no body fat. All day long in that field with no rest, eating what little bread or leaves they had in their pockets. Dawn surmised that even a machine got oiled. The small amount of dirty water they drank from those little dippers could never hydrate their bodies. Until that moment, she never understood the meaning of thirst until she personally experienced May Bee's body's need for water.

The wagon finally stopped at the back door of a beautifully pillared white plantation mansion. Dawn followed close behind May Bee. Each slave woman was counted before being allowed inside by a tall, thin white woman who looked to be in her early fifties. She wore a long white dress with a blue wool shawl wrapped around her shoulders. Dawn could tell she was someone they feared by the way the slave women moved out of her reach. They all, including May Bee, seemed to be in a hurry to get started with whatever they were required to do. Dawn soon figured out she was the wife of the plantation owner. The mistress she was called. A wicked frown covered her face as her blue eyes stared at each woman coming in.

There were women already working in the large plantation home. Dawn watched them dust fixtures, mop floors and do anything else the mistress instructed them to do. There was no kindness in the voice giving orders in a house that felt hotter than the cotton field. Dawn saw her inspect their work holding the blue wool shawl tightly around her shoulders,

"And don't ya'll be stealing my good stuff to take back to them shacks," she snapped.

"Yuh'sum," each voice said in unison as they continued to work with her hovering over them to make sure everything was done to her satisfaction.

After the mistress watched them wash up, May Bee and the others were quickly herded into a large kitchen where they began to cook.

Dawn turned her attention to the young slave girl whose baby had been trampled to death. Blood soiled the front of her half-torn dress. Dawn wondered how she managed to keep busy with her baby's death on her mind. She wouldn't be getting any sympathy anyway. For sure, Dawn could see it wouldn't be coming from the mistress of this plantation. She looked with disdain at all the women—working free for her.

May Bee fried chicken in a large skillet on the mistress's wood stove. They worked for hours in the hot kitchen preparing the food that had been laid out for them to cook. The mistress came in often to inspect and show her dislike for the slaves cooking her food.

It began to smell so good, Dawn wondered how May Bee and the other women would go about getting to eat some of the food they were cooking.

When it was finished, Dawn watched them carry large platters of chicken, roast beef covered with thick gravy, and chunks of baked ham to the spacious dining room where the mistress sat. Mashed potatoes and shelled peas completed her fine meal. A beautiful white cake covered with pecans was placed on the table. The mistress picked over the nibbles of food she placed on her plate.

Dawn was sure the slaves would be offered the leftovers. She knew it wouldn't matter that it was leftover—not as hungry as May Bee's stomach felt. The mistress, she thought, had to have known the women had eaten next to nothing all day. They had been in the cotton fields since before daybreak, with no time to prepare a meal—not even for the children.

After all the food was brought in, the mistress summoned the slave women to stand around the table as she ate alone.

"The master will be in town tonight and won't return to the plantation until the next morning," the mistress informed an old male slave as she continued to pick over her food.

He was dressed more neatly than any of the other slaves. Dawn later learned from May Bee that the mistress had brought him to the plantation when she married the judge. He had been a slave to the mistress when she was a child and now lived in her plantation house with a female slave. No other slaves were allowed inside after their work was done. Many of the female slaves, Dawn was later informed, had never entered the house and worked only in the fields alongside the male slaves.

Dawn watched the mistress teasingly play with the food on her plate and asked, "When do you get to eat May Bee?"

The hunger pangs in the slave woman's stomach made Dawn weak but May Bee never uttered a word. As she moved closer to the mistress, May Bee placed something in her mouth as did the other women. Dawn remembered the bitter taste of the leaves May Bee chewed. Though she no longer felt weak, the leaves didn't ease her hunger.

"Carry them leftovers out to my dogs and don't you dare take a bit of it! I want them fed before the master comes in tomorrow morning. You hear me?" Each slave nodded.

Right before the Mistress rose, May Bee moved behind her chair and exchanged aprons with the woman behind her. Dawn watched that woman give May Bee's apron to the woman behind her and that woman then gave it to the woman behind her. A process the mistress didn't see.

"Come here, May Bee, let me search your apron. I believe you may be putting some of my food in your apron to feed them tainted messes you got."

Dawn knew the mistress meant that May Bee was stealing food to feed her babies—her and the master's babies.

She watched the woman wearing May Bee's apron move behind the other women as they all stood there while May Bee was searched.

"You musta' known I would search you and decided not to steal nothing this time."

After the kitchen was cleaned spotlessly, the mistress marched the women outside with the leftover food to a fenced enclosure where three bloodhounds were making a horrible barking racket. At that moment it occurred to Dawn that the slaves wouldn't be getting any of the festive leftovers.

This witch couldn't be heartless enough to throw to the dogs the food these starving women and their babies could be eating! Sadness consumed Dawn as she listened to the mistress order them to dump the food over the fence. Her stomach rolling over as May Bee's hunger attacked her body. She looked into the cold blue eyes of the mistress and realized the actions she witnessed that day, nearly two centuries before her birth, created for all Americans an unforgivable history with consequences that plague America today. History written in very few history books—none of which she had ever read.

"Head on back to your shacks. I'll see you wenches come cleaning time tomorrow." The smell of the food thrown into the dogs' pen assaulted Dawn's nostrils as her understanding of what had just transpired clayed her mind. The women stumbled out to the waiting wagon to return to their shacks.

As Dawn stood watching them scramble to fix food she wondered, in a world like this, how that catfish thought she would be able to find a way to help May Bee keep her babies. Plus, she only had a few days to get it done. There was no way it would be possible with a woman as cold-hearted as the mistress of that plantation. Tears streamed down her cheeks, not for the poor starving women, but for her own tragic awakening.

May Bee filled the pot outside her shack with water brought back by the slave driving the wagon. The pot served as the cooking utensil for all the slaves on her row. As May Bee began to pull up plants from the small garden beside her shack, Dawn watched the other women add to the pot with different plants they brought from their small gardens. The woman who had ended up with May Bee's apron emptied its contents into the pot of cooking vegetables. Soon the smell of meat had the slaves smiling.

Dawn later learned how dangerous it was to be discovered with any food from the plantation house. If the mistress had discovered meat in May Bee's apron she would have been severely beaten. The many scars covering her body she shared, had come from such beatings.

All the slaves ate outside together. Each took food from the pot with a stick shaped like a spoon. The men ate first, the children were then fed. The women ate what was left. Dawn wondered how it was done in the winter time.

Dawn followed May Bee into another shack. Women stood around the mother of the trampled infant. She sat nursing a baby that apparently belonged to another slave woman. Tears flowed from her eyes as the women gathered in a circle rubbing her arms and back humming a song Dawn had never heard before. That lasted until the baby was fed and the woman laid on the pallet of straw with her body convulsing from the pain of the cruel and brutal death of her baby.

The Unexpected

60

CHAPTER FIVE

DAY TWO

Before daylight Tuesday morning, Dawn watched May Bee rise and dress her babies to be cared for by the older women while she worked in the field and cleaned the house. With her babies in her arms, she looked down at Dawn as if waiting for her to get up just like the previous morning.

"Ya thanking on how to help me keep me babies?"

"Yes, I am May Bee, but can't we miss one day of working in that cotton field. It seems to me after all the work you did yesterday that slave master of yours would give you a day off. That damn sun out in the field is too hot for anyone to work in, not to mention that hot ass kitchen you have to slave in."

"Ya wont May Bee to be stomped in da ground like that po' baby yesdida?"

Dawn closed her eyes, not wanting to think about the events that occurred the day before.

61

"May Bee, the master is sleeping with you and telling you all of his business. He wouldn't harm you when he's got you taking care of his property and needs to visit your bed."

She wondered how she stood his disgusting performance. What was worse he stayed over talking half the night and then fell asleep snoring until he woke up and left. He often didn't leave until the next morning just before it was time for May Bee to go to the field. She and May Bee had watched his wife look from her bedroom window at May Bee's row of shacks. Though Dawn had not been able to make out his features she watched him slowly walk towards the plantation house as his wife looked down at him. Dawn and May Bee knew there would be no consequences his wife could demand. That to Dawn was its own form of enslavement.

"Soon the massa will see fit to sell May Bee and hur babies like he done dem 'fore hur. Come, bes us git gon' fo' day catch May Bee not in dat field wurkin."

She reluctantly struggled up and hurried after May Bee so she wouldn't be late.

Dawn dreaded the time when the sun would be high in the sky draining the water out of every living body moving in that cotton field. The only available water for them would be the same as the day before, unclean having been used by everyone drinking out of one dipper. Like May Bee, rags covered the heads of the slaves careful enough to remember how those rags help save them from the sun that would quickly blister their skin.

Dawn watched the young slave girl who lost her baby to the foot of the overseer's horse take a piece of cotton and wipe blood that ran down her leg. She realized that the slave girl's body had not yet emptied itself of the residue of her pregnancy. The sound of the whip across her back caught Dawn by surprise as everyone looked up. The bloody cotton ball dropped to the ground as the slave girl reached to feel blood running from her back.

"That's the master's cotton ya ruined wench!" More blood ran down her leg, but she ignored it and the open wound caused by the whip. It seemed to Dawn that he was keeping a close watch on her to make sure there wasn't another one of his babies to trample to death.

Just after the sun completed its presence, a horse-drawn carriage rode up and stopped in the cotton field. Dawn moved closer to May Bee. She knew the heavy set, blonde-haired white man seated in the carriage must be someone important because all the slaves stopped working and looked up. He wore a black derby the same as the slave who drove him. His fat, red face was hidden behind a pair of thick rimless glasses. A foot-long beard covered his face. Dawn looked closely at the stout man as he stood up in the carriage. The slave who had driven him stood to hold an umbrella over the man's head. His keen blue eyes stared hard at the overseer who had stomped the baby to death the day before.

"Tell me you done away with a bit of my property yesterday," the man said. Dawn's eyes stretched wide as she looked and listened.

"Don't know what ya speakin' bout sur," the overseer said.

"That baby you stomped into the ground was my valuable property." Dawn's eyes stretched as her mouth opened wide.

"That's the man who's been coming to see you at night, May Bee isn't it?"

May Bee nodded yes.

Dawn thought to herself, *I'd recognize that abrasive voice anywhere.* She still felt that beard scratching her face and his fat body pressing into May Bee's chest and stomach.

"Had no business with it out hare," the overseer said his eyes on the young slave girl. Dawn stared at the blood still dripping from her back and down her legs.

"She needs to be whipped," the overseer stated. "Just waitin' til ya returned to git it done."

"You do realize that female baby wench you killed would have given me at least fifteen more hands once she came of mating age? Plus, the labor she would have provided herself."

Her mouth gaped open as Dawn listened closely to the conversation as the two men stared at each other until the plantation owner spoke again.

"A poor man doesn't have the knowledge in matters of money as does a rich man with wealth and property. Wealth you will no doubt ever obtain being so careless in the handling of another man's property." As he spoke, he glanced over at the slave girl's bloody body.

Stunned by what the plantation owner was telling the overseer, Dawn moved closer to hear what would come next from his lips. The two men's blue eyes locked.

The plantation owner held up a small notepad.

"From my calculations, that comes to five thousand dollars over the estimated years of her life, not including those future hands I lost by your careless killing. Unless you have that amount presently, I must immediately ask for your dismissal." Dawn's eyes popped open even wider as she watched the two men stare each other down. If the overseer didn't have the money the plantation owner asked for, he would be a penniless white man unable to make babies to kill. He would become like all the other white men wandering around stealing food from the crops grown on plantation owners' lands. May Bee had shared as much as they watched two shirtless white men running away from the plantation the day before with corn and melons under their arms.

Those men had no jobs because of free slave labor. That she *did* learn from American History 101. It seemed strange to see it all play out. The overseer never moved. He simply stared at the plantation owner who sounded clearly upset.

Dawn had listened to the plantation owner and May Bee discussing it the night before. May Bee was the source of information about the loss of his property born the day before. *Damn,* she thought. May Bee had more power on that corn shuck pallet than she realized.

"Since that appears to be the case, kindly remove yourself from my horse. Return to me my whip and gun this instant." The overseer lifted his hand and placed it on the gun holster never breaking his stare.

"You'll get no further than my last cotton field before the other overseers have my slaves unleash the hounds on you as though you were a rabbit. They will tear your ass to shreds."

The gun in the holster of the *plantation owner* came up and out.

"No man destroys my property without my permission, especially when they're too poor to compensate my loss!"

Dawn watched in shock as the overseer slid from the horse releasing the gun belt. It dropped on the ground along with the whip. Dawn rejoiced as she watched him hurry down the same path as the men running with the stolen melons and corn.

"Get the hell back to work! Missed time is money," the plantation owner ordered the slaves who stood watching the action. He then directed the slave holding the umbrella to fetch the overseer's gun and whip and secure the horse to the back of the carriage. When he was done, they rode off with no further instructions.

Though Dawn was taken aback by the turn of events, she caught the look of happiness in the eyes of the slaves, especially the young girl whose baby lay dead somewhere under the cotton growing in that plantation field. Someone placed a rag over her wound as she began again to pick her master's cotton.

"Meow, did you see what just happened? This is history in the making."

"Gurlfriend, de plantation massa is de law on his land. Nobody challenges him when it comes to what happen hare. While thay could git 'em an overseer worst, he woulda got de news 'bout what happen to de last overseer from dem ones still workin' fo de plantation massa. Dat would be 'nough fo' him to thank twice 'fo destroyin' de massa's prop'ty. Didn't Meow tell ya thares much t' learn. Ya stays close t' May Bee's side and ya'll learn 'nough to lay t' rest any doubts as to yer knowin' 'bout de life of de female slave in dis country."

Dawn was about to tell the catfish she had enough information for her report, but its voice faded, and she knew it was gone.

When they climbed aboard the wagon, Dawn shook her head in sadness at the others left to work in the scorching hot sun. Hot as Dawn knew it would be inside the house, she was glad to get out of that burning heat. The mistress stood at her back door wrapped in a white wool shawl. Her eyes suspiciously fastened on each slave women who passed, suspecting they had already stolen something. After cleaning themselves up, May Bee and the other slave women went immediately into the kitchen and began pulling out pots and pans. The mistress followed May Bee.

"Where're those babies of yours, black wench? Tell me those white looking babies are fathered by the owner of this plantation."

Dawn moved closer to May Bee as if to protect her from the mistress. She knew she had seen her husband come out of May Bee's shack just that morning.

"They won't be round for long though. I'll see to it that they are sold the first chance I get. Just like I sold the others. Just waiting to hear of someone wanting to buy those tainted messes."

Dawn could see the glee in the mistress's eyes as she watched May Bee tear up. She wondered how the hell the mistress thought May Bee's blood tainted those white babies. All her husband had to do to keep his family pure and untainted was to keep his penis inside his own race of women.

"Poor white men can't rest for you black wenches pulling them into your shacks."

"What! Is she serious May Bee?"

May Bee didn't answer Dawn. She instead directed her words to the mistress, "I done los' de res'. Let May Bee have some love. Dese all I got to love."

Tears dripped down her dark cheeks. Dawn stared at the mistress with hatred as she felt the depth of May Bee's pain.

"Well, too damn bad!" the mistress screeched. You're not human you're a slave, wench. How do you know what love is? You already had two of yours sold. What's two more gonna matter?"

"Whare's God when ya need 'em? Even de ol' cow loves da babies same as I love dese dats' mines."

"God is not going to help no slave find anything to love! That's for sure," the mistress scowled. If it wasn't for you wenches seducing our white men, I wouldn't have lost my two babies. They never made it into this world."

Dawn closed her eyes as she shook her head thinking to herself, the mistress had to be crazy to brainwash herself to believe that sick, starved, frail, exhausted, burned, whipped and raped slave women had the strength, or desire, to seduce her husband.

"That's because her body was unable to carry them to full term," Dawn said sucking in her breath. "Don't believe her lies, May Bee. Your body did nothing to destroy the babies she lost. It's not your fault she can't keep her husband in her own bed." Dawn said staring at the Mistress in disgust.

She wanted to speak for May Bee but knew it was impossible. The mistress devalued the lives of all the slaves on her plantation especially the female slaves. To her, they were less than all the plantation animals she provided with food and care. Her knowledge that her husband desired her body less than he did the female slaves she considered animals seared hatred into her heart.

Dawn saw the look of hate in her eyes. She believed it had to have come from her inability to stop her husband's rampant infidelity. Those half-white babies were clear evidence of the slave master's *unquenchable* thirst for the bodies of his female slaves. Dawn soon discovered that May Bee was one of many female slaves who served the master's sexual needs.

Her thoughts went back to the beautiful bed she glimpsed when May Bee was told to bring down sheets from the mistress's finely appointed bedroom. The mistress's bed looked more desirable than her own bed at home. Pink and red roses covered the wide bedspread and huge pillows lay against the tufted headboard. One press of the hand and the mattress sprang right back up. Dawn couldn't imagine what could possibly be in a female slave's shack that so enticed a man with the ability to sleep in a bed as beautiful as this? A man who preferred having sex on straw and corn shucks with a slave. Didn't he care what mental trauma that caused his wife?

CHAPTER SIX

DAWN

Dawn slept next to May Bee and her babies that third night after another bizarre day. She peeped out through the cracks between May Bee's shack hopeful another snake wouldn't crawl through. Her thoughts roamed as she reflected a year ago when she had taken a Sociology class that dealt with the social order of slave life in America. The professor was said to be, not only personally eccentric, but also strange in the way he taught his classes. He could recite every word in some 33 books. Any assignment he was questioned about, he could tell the student the page number and the line of the subject matter, and of course, explain the message the author wanted to convey.

The oddest thing she discovered about the professor was that he sat on the floor of his classroom and by the third day required his students to do the same. It was possible to get a *C* out of his class if you were lucky. Dawn had been warned that most of his students dropped out before the semester ended, but she decided to take the class anyway and accept the *C* as a passing grade and worry about *A's* and *B's* in law school. It didn't bother Dawn that her 4.0 average would drop; she needed the class.

The first day she saw him, his wiry blonde hair flew everywhere. A mustache covered the lips of the professor. She estimated his age as early sixties. Tall and lanky, it didn't seem to Dawn that he knew much of anything although his wide brown eyes appeared to read her thoughts. His first requirement shocked the class. The syllabus required that they read *Uncle Tom's Cabin* by Harriet Beecher Stowe. Before they could read the book, he informed them that they must first learn to understand the language so that they better understood the people the author wrote about. His course was not about slavery and its woes but about the language the captive people taught themselves in order to communicate with those who enslaved them. A language that had been developed "Within the Clamor of Chains." This he wrote on chart paper in bold letters.

He taught that the language the slaves used was not only important because of how it was developed, but also because it was purposely coded to conceal information they desired to withhold from the plantation owners and overseers. He went on to say that the captive people were

74

forced to develop a coded language because of the violence used to control their lives. The students were required to decode the language spoken in Stowe's novel. Dawn had flipped through the book shaking her head.

Early in the course, the professor was criticized by a white male student who refused to participate. He argued that those *dis's* and *da's* were so unacceptable that no one cared to learn them much less learn the meanings they conveyed. If there were some meanings to decode, they were of no value to him.

The professor stopped his lecture and cautiously explained, "What one believes has no value may prove to be the most valuable over time. That is why you must always prepare for the unexpected, son."

"African American students surely don't value those slave nigger utterances!" the student shouted at him. She and her classmates sat looking at him in shock as they watched him gather his books.

"Why," he added, "should I trouble myself with decoding their poor ass English?"

He lashed out calling the professor an old, stupid fool. "I'm certainly not your son," he finished with a final insult before storming out of the classroom. Dawn had been glad there were no black students taking the course.

As soon as a B flashed up as her grade, Dawn dismissed what the professor had taught them. Her feelings were the same as the outraged student at the time; she believed nothing he taught was of any value to her. Dawn just wanted to get a passing grade so that she could enter law school. As far as she was concerned, what he taught occurred in some distant past. Nothing important to her as a white girl.

There were no black friends in Dawn's life. Most certainly, no black people she cared about. She never thought of the eccentric professor again until just this moment. Here she lay in 1842 in America next to an African slave woman and her babies on a corn shuck pallet. People she definitely cared about. There was so much she could have learned from that professor, but believing he could not teach her anything impactful, she had not prepared herself for the *unexpected*.

Dawn moved closer to May Bee hopeful the plantation owner wouldn't come again that night. Sadness filled her heart for the slave woman and her babies. According to the historical slavery timeline, May Bee faced an entire lifetime of enslavement even her babies would never be truly free. There was nothing she could compare to this. May Bee's life was as real to her as her own life and she couldn't imagine being born into a world where her life belonged to someone else. It seemed unthinkable that a time existed in America where a woman's children were born belonging to another person who had the *right* to sell them *at will.*

How could this type of slavery be justified by civilized people? She had read about it, but living it became an entirely different matter. No woman in her lifetime, black or white, could have endured even one day of slave life! Without the magic of that catfish, she would not have survived one hour working out in that hot sun baking her brain and body to death. Some unexpected fluke had placed her there. *For what purpose?* She didn't know but nothing in her wildest dreams had prepared her for what she had already witnessed. She couldn't fathom anything worse.

Dawn wondered how Tony would address the class on *"The Life of The Slave Female."* She turned her thoughts to Tony's fair skin color. There were many half white people on this plantation—young and old. Some as fair as Tony; others as white as she. The only thing that made it apparent that they were not pure white was the fact that their birth came about on this plantation by a female slave. That knowledge alone sealed their fate forever. Unless they escaped to where no one knew them they were doomed to live the life of slavery just as the dark-skinned slaves. Lighter skin did nothing to alter their fate in this barbaric world.

Dawn remembered hearing that lighter-skinned Blacks received preferential treatment. Not on this plantation. Except for the mistress's two very dark-skinned house slaves, all other slaves had to work the fields. They all received the same treatment. Since most were born on the plantation they had no idea what existed beyond it. She observed a society that made no sense to her and lessons she learned in the professor's classroom spun around in her head. In the minds of the slave masters, they feared that the men and women they enslaved might someday—or night— demand their human rights and *retribution*! This fear was wide spread in the white man's mind the professor taught. The existence of this fear left no doubt that the slave masters knew that those captive men and women were as *human* as they.

If African slaves had lost their human traits during the middle passage and become like animals, as the white man asserted in defense of his barbaric behavior, his insatiable sexual appetite soon saw to it that they received some of his human traits in exchange. Those very babies who carried his genes would one day *damn* him and demand their human rights. The professor's teachings were often quite unpopular with the young white students.

This term she sat in class with students examining her knowledge of American history and her *fabrication* of slavery atrocities. It wasn't until this class that she concerned herself with the fact that many African people who live in this country arrived as *immigrants*. Their cultural background was not the same as the black Americans whose ancestors had lived in this country as slaves. They shared only skin, Tony had assured her. She believed slaves lived marginal lives but not the horrors that Tony, Shirley, Tina and those books they *insisted* she read depicted. They made it appear as if *she* had profited from those horrors. To them, she was a privileged white girl whose life was protected by the establishment. Dawn needed this class and she was not going to be discouraged by confrontational outbursts.

The class instructions stated that every student would write a report on some aspect of American history that occurred in the 16th through the 19th centuries. The class had become troublesome and unruly for the instructor whose syllabus didn't suit all the students.

Some students insisted that the book they were studying didn't detail a true and accurate account of every American during that time in history. Other students, and the white instructor, insisted that it did indeed tell the complete story. Dawn reasoned that Tony, Shirley, and Tina simply wanted sympathy. There were four other black students in the classroom—the African exchange students who never commented on the accuracy of what had been written in the history books. She guessed because it never gave details about their part in the introduction of slavery into the Western world.

She felt determined to prove Tony, Shirley, and Tina wrong in their assessment of American history and the treatment of their ancestors. Dawn *remembered* the instructor asking where they were in the syllabus the second week of class. He turned pages as if to find a point of reference. He seemed confused but Dawn surmised that he was sure of the text but knew the loaded debates it would evoke between the white and black students. The class atmosphere and debates over slave history rushed back to Dawn's mind. She was embarrassed by her apparent ignorance.

Shirley, a tall, thin, dark-skinned student wore *dreads* that hung down to her waist. Tina stood short and wide-hipped; her skin the color of a brown paper bag. She wore her hair the same as Tony's in a wide natural that sprang out six inches from her head. A basketball player,

Tony stood 6'4." Because he was fair skinned, he always spoke of himself as being whitewashed and was known for his verbal outbursts usually spoken when confronting white Americans.

"We stopped when Tony stated that the first Africans coming into this country came from the Congo and were bonded servants who had to work seven years before gaining their freedom. Indentured service that even white servants were a part of," Dawn informed the class.

"I also stated," Tony said rising, "that Africans who came by way of the middle passage as the cargo of slave traders were worked as free labor until they died, rarely able to gain their freedom."

"Are you sure it wasn't that they were brought over to this *Christian* country to save them from their barbaric life in Africa?" Dawn questioned. "Look around you, Tony, there are more Africans coming to America than there are African Americans going back to Africa. It seems to me that if what you are telling the class is true that wouldn't be the case," Dawn argued.

Tony scowled and Dawn went on.

"Don't forget it was other Africans who went deep into the jungle kidnapping Africans to sell to the British. No white soldiers could have gone that far into the jungle with those wild animals and thick brush to bring all those black people out. Isn't that how they became slaves in America in the first place? Wonder what those African brothers were paid for selling your ancestors? It couldn't have been very much because they sure don't have it now, do they?" The white students laughed.

The mouths of all the black students fell open.

"You need to include them and not act as if only white people participated in your enslavement. We sure don't want to let your brother and sister Africans off the hook now do we? It's called giving complete and accurate details, Tony."

"Tell 'em, Miss Perry Mason, we sure don't want to leave out the Africans who sold them in the first place do we?" a white male student shouted out as other white students applauded.

Smiling at Tony with confidence, Dawn noticed that the African exchange students seemed to shrink in their seats. She felt totally in control of the debate until Shirley jumped in.

"Yeah, like what was written in that Texas high school textbook that stated we *migrated* from Africa like other migrants who came over looking for a better life. That's the history everyone is programmed to believe."

"I believe, Shirley," Dawn replied, "that was a rare error that occurs from time to time even in the most thoroughly written textbooks. It's called an oversight."

"An oversight, Dawn," Tina shot back as the rest of the students turned to her, "is what you white folks call it when you are caught lying. You know what I mean? Like when you purposely leave out the truth."

"Like I said, an oversight." Dawn frowned as Tina poked holes into what she felt were facts.

"There were at least three land rushes after the Civil War," Tina said. "A war that black soldiers gave their lives to help win if you don't recall."

"What do land rushes have to do with what we are studying?" Dawn asked irritated that *they* were spoiling her enjoyment of this class.

"One was in 1885, another in 1889, and the largest was the Oklahoma Land Rush of 1893. How many ex-slaves were allowed the opportunity to rush for land that should have been *given* to them? We aren't even going to mention those mules you promised but never delivered. One of many of the white man's broken promises."

Dawn opened her mouth in rebuttal, but Tina wasn't finished.

"Let's talk about the freedom the slaves fought and died for only to be compensated with Jim Crow laws that further destroyed their lives."

Her hands placed on her thin hips, Shirley, a history major interjected, "The Native Americans don't call them oversights; they call them broken treaties."

"Amen!" Tony, Tina and the Asian students said in unison.

"How many Europeans did you allow to rush for land when they came to this country? Did *they* help you win the Revolutionary War you joyfully celebrate on the Fourth of July? And what about the Civil War our ancestors helped A-mer-i-ca win?" Shirley said with the conviction of truth in her voice.

"Yet those white immigrants were given land that should have been given to the freed slaves. Not one free slave got anything but a damn rope around their neck after they helped you win *two* wars and worked two hundred and fifty years for free! You're just conceited liars!"

To further Dawn's discomfort, Tony took up the berating.

"You don't know the truth about our history. You don't even know the truth about your own history except for the lies you have been told to make you feel less guilty about what our ancestors went through at the hands of your ancestors."

"Bullshit lies!" Dawn shot back. "We saved your African asses from a brutal life in the jungle. Admit it! You're glad to be on this good American soil or your asses would have run back to Africa lickety-split." Laughter rolled from the white students.

"I don't see you running back to Europe to those caves you dwelled in for centuries. Troglodytes!" Shirley shouted.

"And what about those prisons you left to come here in order to escape death by hanging?" Tina's voice rang out.

"Class quiet down!" the instructor finally called out nervously. The debate was growing out of his comfort zone. "Calm down, we are all adults here! I need you to control your outbursts and simply follow the syllabus. Your reports must be factual and within the designated time period. The class has challenged Tony and Dawn to an oral report on the life of the female slave. Think you two are up to the challenge? The class can then have an open discussion on the slave woman's life in America."

What about it, Dawn?" Tony asked.

"Sure, why not, her life couldn't have been that bad." Her smugness was evident.

"Where is God when you need Him?" Tony asked shaking his head in disbelief. "A time machine is what this white female needs to take her ass back in time to experience life as a female slave!" he shouted.

"Believe me, I'm ready for God and your time machine just to prove your black ass wrong!"

At the time Dawn wasn't sure how she was going to find the needed information, but his challenge didn't scare her. Laughter sounded throughout the classroom. She and Tony gave each other menacing looks as they gathered their books. Soon the classroom was empty.

Here she lay, devoid of all smugness, beside a slave woman and her babies wondering what else she would learn. The sound of May Bee's snores reminded Dawn that before long an alarm would go off in the slave woman's brain and she would rise speaking to her in a dialect so different from her own. She never gave American slave dialect much thought despite the eccentric professor's urging. Here living with May Bee, she couldn't imagine how long it must have taken these slaves struggling with physical violence, hunger and other atrocities to understand a language as difficult as English. Though some had lived on this plantation several generations, none spoke English without difficulty. The sociology professor believed had their native language been preserved, one could have easily identified from where most slaves originated. It was too bad, he shared, that the dialect they spoke would be frowned upon by future generations of their own people, unaware of the importance of its formation within in the *clamor of chains*.

This was American history she never understood. It was a part of history that never touched her life. As a white woman she knew slavery occurred but never to the cruel extent she now witnessed. She couldn't believe she supported people who found ways to minimize the existence of this horrible institution. No wonder the truth of slavery for the female slave was so erroneously slanted in the history books. Living it decried all understanding and no one would believe this kind of cruelty was endured by any woman.

The mistresses of these plantations were white women bound by their own set of chains. Dawn imagined being a young bride married to a judge; the envy of all her friends and adored by relatives who believed she had gotten the best catch possible. Soon after she becomes pregnant, she loses her baby and discovers a slave woman has given birth to a baby who looks just like her husband. She sees other slave children who look to be his as well; something that continued throughout their marriage. She had to live with the fact that his penis had entered those female slave bodies just as it had entered hers. Two people couldn't get any closer than that. Her husband was that close to female slaves before and after he was that close to her. What a mind-boggling discovery. She couldn't leave him. What man would have her? Would her life be any different? She was his property thus powerless to stop her husband from being unfaithful to her, forced to live with the legacy of his infidelity; bound to the fact that she must share her husband's body with the *slaves* he *craved* sexual relations with. His wealth was the law and he dictated whose life mattered on his land.

In order to survive that mental anguish, she made believe her husband was a victim. Shifting the blame of those sexual encounters and pregnancies onto the slave women *seductresses*. Selling their babies as punishment. That kind of mind-altering seemed too impossible for any sane person to believe. Dawn was ashamed to learn her female ancestors were that gullible and cruel. She shook her head as she thought of the insanity that existed in this century. She could no longer live in denial.

Whatever genius the slave possessed was plundered and destroyed under the belief that only the white man's knowledge held value. She had learned that from the odd professor who had carefully studied his own race of men during that period in history and shared the unwelcome knowledge with students who refused to open their minds to those facts.

If she could, she would seek out the professor and ask him where were the men and women who should have prevented the African men and women from being brought into this country? All white men were not slave owners. Those who were educated, intelligent people surely should have decried the wretched horrors going on around them. Some of those men had to have been sane unless, of course, insanity was indeed *contagious*. May Bee wanted to keep her babies from being sold by the mistress. That catfish must be out of its fool mind to think she could persuade the mistress to do anything—she couldn't even talk to her! Dawn remembered listening to the mistress berate a slave woman after she accused her of stealing a red scarf. When another slave pointed to the scarf on a chair, the mistress hurried to tell the slave woman of its value. The scarf, she cautioned her, was made of pure wool and since she was not human, she could not conceive of its value. Not once did she think it necessary to make amends for calling the woman a thief.

"'I no like. It's ugli. I no take like ya say,' the poor slave woman said in her own defense.

The eyes of the mistress enlarged with rage and Dawn watched her snatch her cattails from a nearby hook and whip the slave woman for having the nerve to utter any dislikes. Dawn's heart went out to the woman who simply wanted her owner to know she was not a thief.

Dawn watched the mistress unfold the scarf and wrap it around the head of the slave woman, "You better wear it every day you come into this house!" she cackled in delight at her cruel entertainment. It was hot that day and Dawn wondered how the mistress endured wearing her own wool covering. The slave woman didn't want that hot wool around her head, but she learned too late that telling her owner what she didn't like would be exactly what she got – along with the scars from the cattails. As hard as Dawn tried, she couldn't sleep on May Bee's corn shuck pallet that night. The stars blinked at Dawn and she blinked back at their brightness. After a deep sigh, it crossed her mind that her parents had probably called to check on her and she couldn't be reached. They would be worried and return home sooner than planned. Then it occurred to Dawn that Meow had worked things out so she wouldn't be missed. She was glad of that because this was an adventure she would never forget.

Dawn thought about what had occurred when they went to pick up May Bee's children from the old women's

90

shack. It was seldom that May Bee talked. When they returned to her shack after the mistress threatened her with the sale of her two babies, May Bee's heart weighed heavily. She worried that the mistress would soon make good on her sadistic plan. May Bee lay on her sack bed crying. She cried so loudly Dawn stroked her hoping the sleeping babies wouldn't wake up.

"May Bee, this life you are forced to live will one day be a disgrace. If I could, I would take you back with me to a place where no one could sell your babies. They would be yours forever, May Bee." Dawn watched a look of disbelief unfold across May Bee's face.

"It's true May Bee. Where I am from no man has the right to put babies in you unless you want him to. There are no masters or mistresses who own any woman or man." Dawn stopped to clarify. "Well, not in this country. I can't speak for the entire planet."

"Wha' ya sa?" May Bee asked as she wiped at the tears that wet her face.

"May Bee, your world is as crazy as the people controlling it." May Bee's eyes stretched.

"Where I'm from people marry who they love no matter their color." Dawn touched May Bee's arm. "Women with skin the color of yours marry men with the color of mine all the time. Their babies are safe with them and nobody takes and sells them."

"Wha' heben is dat?" Her question stunned Dawn.

"A heaven, May Bee, where women are free to speak their minds no matter their skin color and babies belong to the women who birth them."

"May Bee ain't seed dat heben jes dis place whare me and dese babies is." May Bee cried on and off throughout the night.

Normality for the descendants of slaves was far removed from what their female ancestors were forced to endure. It was like viewing two different species of females. She could never truly explain to May Bee the end results of slavery. What she had already told her seemed some made up fantasy that comes only from impossible dreams. The words of the outraged student flooded Dawn's mind. What if it were possible to take May Bee back with her? Most important was how would her descendants embrace her?

CHAPTER SEVEN

DAY THREE

Dawn watched the sun kiss the earth that Wednesday morning as it rose and lured night into day. Soon it would become unbearably hot. Three more days. Could she make it? If only she didn't have to stand with May Bee out in the sun until midday. A look of surprise covered her face when she saw the slave who came for them in the afternoon drive up early that morning just after daybreak. The same slave who had come for them the two previous afternoons in the cotton field came that *morning* instead. Dawn couldn't believe her luck as she followed the slave women who dropped their sacks on the ground and hurried aboard.

Once they arrived at the plantation house, she looked along with the other women at a horse-drawn carriage that rode up in front about the same time as they did. No one climbed down from the wagon. The mistress's female house slave rushed out to help two young white girls, step from inside the carriage. The tails of their wide petticoat dresses danced around their ankles. The large fans in their hands sprang open as they began to fan themselves causing the feathers on their wide-brimmed hats to flutter.

A male slave stepped out of a small dwelling next to the plantation house and approached the driver of the carriage. Dawn remembered he was the slave who had driven the plantation owner to the cotton field the day before.

"Wonda' whare's Ol' Joe?" the slave woman wearing the mistress's red wool scarf asked from the wagon they were seated in. Dawn watched the carriage driver say something to the man who came out from the small shack. They exchanged hand signs. The carriage driver then slapped his hand against his chest.

A slave woman looking at the none verbal exchange between the two men shouted, "Ol' Joe don' gone' to glory ya'll."

The male slave driving the wagon raised his hand and nodded his head. Dawn reflected on the odd professor. There had been some kind of communication going on among the slaves. Though what they communicated remained a mystery to her, the smiles on the slave women's faces indicated to Dawn they understood that nonverbal language.

After the mistress watched the female slaves come in through the back door, she ordered that lemonade be served to her guests. Dawn watched the girls settle in the parlor as they sipped from the glasses of lemonade offered. She then saw the mistress's eyes narrow as she looked at the girls.

"I see Ol' Joe ain't out there. What have my nieces been up to?" she asked suspiciously. Both girls covered their lips. Their fans switched back and forth.

Her blonde ringlets whirling the older niece, giggled.

"Well, I hate to tell you, Aunt Martha," said the younger niece as she pushed her long brown hair behind her back. "Cherry had Ol' Joe hung."

Dawn watched the mistress's lips slack. Her eyes stretched as she shook her head.

"I do declare Cherry, what could Ol' Joe have possibly done for you to have him hung?" Dawn moved closer to the parlor door to better hear the conversation.

"Well," said Cherry as she began to fan herself, "you know very well male slaves ain't allowed to look at a white woman directly. It's unbecoming and shows no respect. That ol' nigger looked at me straight in my eyes. He knew better," she said as her ringlets brushed along her shoulders. "I told him to look away, but he just kept staring at me." She tossed her hair and said, "I told daddy he better have him hung right then and there!"

"Why Ol' Joe can't see far as his nose. If it wasn't for his horse, he wouldn't know how to get to the judge's plantation. He rocked you when you were a baby, girl. He probably didn't even know it was you he was looking at."

"Well, he won't have to worry about that now 'cause he's buried with the rest of them dead nigger slaves," Cherry said with an air of entitlement.

Oh, my goodness, Dawn thought as her hands covered her lips. No wonder they seemed happy that the male slave was dead. *She had a blind man killed for looking at her. If the man couldn't see, how could he possibly know she's ugly as sin? Reason enough, not to look at her.* Dawn stared at the girl in shame as the mistress continued to question her niece.

"You near sixteen, Cherry. Time now for that brother of mine to seek a husband for you." Her fan moving back and forth, Cherry smiled. "Ain't that many single plantation owners 'round here. Might have to look farther than Louisiana for my husband. I surely don't plan to marry up with these old farts round here. Told daddy I'm not marrying no man less he got slaves. I don't intend to live like poor white crackers that's for sure." Dawn watched her close her fan as she shook her ringlets and cut her eyes at her aunt.

"You gotta know how to control slaves once you become the mistress of a plantation, Cherry. I'm glad to see you don't mind handling niggers that get too uppity. Can't let them think they human like us. Next thing you know they'll be telling you what they ain't gonna do. Something that sho' ain't gonna happen if I got anything to say 'bout it."

Dawn watched the younger niece stand and place her hands on her hips, "Well, when a man marries me, I'm going to take my own slave Toby with me because I love her. She talks to me and takes an interest in what I like."

"Aunt Martha this little sister of mine is only thirteen so she still has feelings for our niggers. She doesn't understand she has to be stern with them, so they know their place."

"Why must I treat them any different than I do anyone else, Aunt Martha? They are people just like us, aren't they?"

"Of course not, Mindy!" Laughter rushed from the lips of Cherry and the mistress.

"Why not? My Toby is no different than me. She has everything that I have."

"She's a black nigger wench, Mindy. We can't afford to love a slave, can we Aunt Martha? That's what Momma says."

"Your mother's right Mindy. You will learn soon enough."

"I don't want to learn soon enough. My Toby is in my heart. When I'm sad she sings to me. Toby takes time with me, and Momma is always busy. Anyway, not all slaves are dark, Aunt Martha. Some are as white as we are."

The mistress sat up and held her hand tight against her breasts.

"It don't matter, gal. Their blood is tainted that makes them slaves just like they're black. Toby had some of them tainted babies, but your wise mother sold them down the river just like I did. I'll be selling me some more pretty soon." Dawn's heart sank realizing whose babies she meant.

"What makes some of them so fair and others pure black like Toby, Aunt Martha? Why aren't they all the same color?"

The mistress lips parted but not a word was uttered.

"I just don't understand why we can't all get along, especially when they are taking care of us."

Mindy pressed her fan in front of her dress and sat down again next to her sister. Loud gasps from the lips of the aunt and the older niece could be heard. Dawn waited to hear more. She took a deep breath feeling sad for the young girl who would soon be programmed to think like the adults who controlled her life.

"Don't be a fool," the mistress corrected her niece. "No slave is human like us. And just so you know, we take care of them. Without our care they couldn't make it. Brought them out of those jungles and made Christians out of them."

Damn, thought Dawn, *I used to think just like that.*

The mistress sighed and said to Mindy, "I believe I must have a talk with that sister-in-law of mine. Seems to me, she might need to sell Toby before that nigger wench spoils your ability to think clearly about these slaves."

The fan in Mindy's hand dropped to the floor as she fell to her knees in front of her aunt pleading, "Please, Aunt Martha, please don't tell Momma to sell my Toby. I think I'd about die if she was sold from me. I'll promise not to love her anymore. Please, Aunt Martha don't tell momma to sell her!"

Cherry giggled in delight at the emotional scene and Dawn's eyes watered knowing Toby wouldn't be in Mindy's life for very long if the mistress had any say about it.

"They don't understand what it is to have feelings, Mindy," the mistress shared as her niece sobbed with her head in her aunt's lap. "They can't love like we love. It's not in them to have our emotions. That nigger's just clinging to you cause your momma sold them tainted messes of hers."

Dawn shook her head as she watched the nefarious mistress stroke her niece's back calmly explaining to her that the slaves were their *property* just like the other animals and had to be treated as such.

"They take such poor care of the clothes they are issued twice a year," the mistress said in disgust.

Cherry laughed when she added that the slaves didn't have sense enough to appreciate how clothes given to them should be cared for. She thought every cruelty endured by the slaves was a necessary means of control. The conversation changed as the mistress bragged to her nieces that it wouldn't be long before she and their uncle left the plantation for a trip to Pennsylvania then to Europe. Dawn could see the evidence of free labor all around her as she observed the elaborate lifestyle the plantation owner and his wife enjoyed.

She could also see that the mistress was so indoctrinated by the conditions of slave life she believed they were too dumb to understand her cruelties. She was a woman who couldn't put on her own stockings or underwear without slave help according to May Bee who heard it from the slave woman who lived in the house. She couldn't even put together her outfits or comb her own hair. *How dumb was that?* Dawn thought.

Sunday was the day all the slaves spent time with the slave preacher and each other. For the house slaves, night was the same as day. If the mistress wanted her house slaves up on pretense of illness or work, they were hauled up at any hour and berated until the mistress was satisfied or just too sleepy to keep them up any longer. Whether or not they were allowed Sundays off depended on her needs. Her cruelties didn't go unnoticed nor did her need for them, yet she continuously referred to them as dumb.

The conversation among the aunt and her nieces pulled Dawn's thoughts back to the odd professor and all he tried to teach them. It had been in his class that she learned about slavery in a way that made her feel uncomfortable. She didn't care for his teaching style, but she was curious about his theories of slavery and its perils.

As she stood listening to the mistress and her nieces, Dawn thought of this man who believed the white people in this country had grouped the descendants of slaves together with African immigrants and all other non-white citizens.

The professor's theory was, that because of slavery, descendants of slaves held a unique place in our country. America had failed to give an account for that place and disassociated itself with the responsibility of its tragedies. To white America, slavery was not fully recognized as a major factor in the growth and prosperity of our nation and slave descendants were vaguely acknowledged for their part in that growth.

"Why were they such *bitter* people?" Dawn and her fellow classmates questioned. It was their white *ancestors* who started the institution of slavery, not them. Instead of answering their questions he gave the class a research assignment: *What if there had been no slavery in America? What mental stress did white Americans endure because of slavery?* The Sociology professor bombarded them with questions that required answers they believed couldn't be answered.

Dawn's keen sense of examination searched to find answers to those questions and her final report posed more questions: *What if women, of any race, without husbands were banned from entering the country? What if white men, in the wake of losing their jobs as farm laborers, declared that no cotton could be grown in the south unless each bow was picked by paid hands? Would this country have been as great a nation with paid labor?*

"Slavery," the professor lectured, "crippled the country mentally as well as physically. White men who had recently won their own freedom from the British rule depended on the enslavement of another race to give value to their own lives. Why didn't poor whites understand that slavery damaged their ability to work and take care of their families and fight against it?" he asked. "It served only to destroy the values and principles born out of the fight for independence from British rule. Those principles and values were fought and died for."

Slavery, he taught, became the trickster that locked white Americans into a system that nullified all they cherished about independence. Laws enacted to seal the fate of the Africans enslaved in this country sealed their fate as well. What they believed made them superior transformed them into criminals and hunters of *human* lives. Hatred of people deemed inferior gave justification to squander life and the need to save the savages from a burning hell created a new *American* hell.

The *B* she received from the odd Sociology professor resulted from the questions she asked and answered. It was a grade she didn't expect, but she knew she had written something he thought deserved consideration.

The shrill voice of the mistress brought Dawn back to the 1842 old plantation home.

"Only the blacksmith, the butcher, and the plantation owner's driver are given shoes. It keeps the slaves from getting very far in case they decided to run," she heard the mistress educate her nieces.

Running from the harsh slave life they endured, Dawn thought.

She turned away from the parlor and walked into the kitchen where May Bee and four other women stood preparing lunch for the mistress and her guests. "May Bee did you hear what she said about having that old man hung?"

"Les he be in heben now."

"May Bee!"

"No talk. Thay thank me ain't right in de head talkin' to a ghos'.

Dawn for the first time noticed how strangely the other slave women looked at May Bee. She understood what May Bee meant, sighed and went back to the parlor door. If she couldn't talk to May Bee, she may as well listen to what else the mistress and her nieces had to say.

How to get the mistress to allow May Bee to keep her babies filled Dawn's thoughts. She heard the mistress discuss what she thought the female slave Toby's fate should be. There was no doubt in her mind what the mistress had planned for May Bee's babies.

"I wish we were allowed to go to those mating parties the men attend," Cherry giggled.

"There is going to be one tomorrow here at your plantation, Aunt Martha. I could smell the meat on the pits as we drove up." Cherry's change of subject piqued Dawn's interest.

"Party, what party?" Mindy asked. "I must ask mother if I can come. I love parties." She watched Cherry cover her lips with her fan. The mistress also covered her lips.

"It's too much for the eyes of a lady my husband tells me."

"Well, if I were a wife, I would attend the party just to see what goes on. Especially if my husband was invited. He could not leave me behind and have fun by himself."

"Mindy, your husband would not allow you to attend a party with slaves; it's too harsh for the eyes of a lady. Insisting would be disrespectful of your husband's wishes.

Who but he would know best?" The mistress and Cherry smiled at each other.

"Aunt Martha, I think it's a shame we have to be bound by the wishes of men. Why can't we think for ourselves?" The mistress's lips tightened as she frowned at Mindy.

"No, we cannot. We must listen to the words of our men. Who but they would know what's best for us?" The mistress was angry with insistence.

"Well, I don't really care to go as long as those wenches find mates at that party, so they won't be after our men." Cherry got a nod of agreement from her aunt.

Dawn wondered if Mindy would become one of the few white women of that era to realize she had a mind and must use it to think for herself. Staring at them, Dawn wondered *what would they say if they could see one of their own descendants standing before them?*

She wished they could see her in her shorts and halter. Those hot, floor-length petticoat dresses worn in this heat had to feel awful. She was thankful her ancestors had brains enough to move past that senseless fashion, especially in the summertime.

Dawn watched the slave women serve the mistress and her guests their lunch. Soon after, she was surprised to see May Bee and the others walk towards the outside door. May Bee beckoned her to come and Dawn hurried after them.

Once they left the plantation house, Dawn discovered they wouldn't be returning to the cotton field; they were headed elsewhere. She was relieved not to be going back into that hot sun. *A mating party tomorrow? Sounds like fun*, she thought as she wondered if the female slaves would get to pick their own mates. If so, she was glad. May Bee would no longer have to be impregnated by the plantation master. The problem would be May Bee's ability to find someone she liked. Dawn planned to help her with that.

The smell of food cooking drew her attention. It was meat smoking in open pits on the side of the road. May Bee later told her it was pigs and goats. Cherry had mentioned meat cooking in pits out in the open for the mating party. The driver took them to a large building where they joined other female slaves who stood over huge wood stoves baking cakes and pies. Pots filled with green vegetables were being stirred by the women. Male slaves carried in long tables and placed nicely cushioned chairs under them. The plantation owner stood inside giving directions that were immediately carried out.

Once a year, Dawn learned from May Bee, the plantation owner held a mating party for his female slaves who were not pregnant but had started their *bleeding*. She'd gone with May Bee early that morning to take her babies to be kept by the old slave women. May Bee already informed her that they wouldn't be going to the cotton field the next day. The mating party would be that day and she must attend.

Dawn sighed, thankful for a day's reprieve from the heat of the sun. She wondered why the plantation owner hadn't allowed May Bee to find a mate long before now at the mating parties. Perhaps May Bee was already pregnant by him, who knows. She hoped he would allow her to meet someone this time and not keep her all to himself.

May Bee didn't talk about the party the way Dawn hoped she would, particularly about finding a mate. May Bee was shy and never talked much. She didn't play with her babies the way most mothers do. She'd look at them, cuddle and wash their bodies, but not one word did she speak to them. It was strange, Dawn thought, that she had not even named her babies. May Bee was different from any of the other slave women she watched interact with their children. Taking care of her babies' needs took most of her time when she wasn't working. Dawn would have to wait. There would be time to talk with May Bee once she met a potential mate. He might not be able to see or hear her, but May Bee surely would. She planned to whisper to May Bee if she thought a certain male slave was the right one.

CHAPTER EIGHT
DAY FOUR

"Ya stays. May Bee go by hurself dis 'time." That Thursday morning Dawn sat on the corn shuck pallet peeping out of the crack in May Bee's shack. May Bee sat on her only stool with her hand in the can of vanilla grease rubbing its contents over her body.

"You have insisted I go everywhere with you. Why can't I go with you today?"

"White womins ain't 'llowed to massa's matin' part's no how. Ya' stay put. May Bee be back." She sounded like the mistress. Dawn thought of Mindy's feelings about women learning to think for themselves. Dawn was most certainly one such woman. After all the horrors she had witnessed, she was determined to go to the mating party. She needed to see May Bee have fun for once.

"I'm going, May Bee. Where I come from men don't tell women where they can and can't go." Dawn hurried and slipped on her Nikes.

Before May Bee could respond, the shack door opened. Dawn looked shocked to see three familiar overseers scurry inside and tell May Bee she must come with them. They hurried her out of the shack with Dawn close behind.

Lines of wagons filled with female slaves stood outside. Familiar and unfamiliar White men stood beside them. *Where were the males the women would choose from?* Dawn wondered. She guessed they couldn't call them possible husbands because the men could be sold away from the women any time the slave master decided. Dawn watched other slave women on May Bee's shack row climb aboard the wagons.

The wagons were driven to the large building they were at the previous day. Dawn sat beside May Bee in expectation. Remembering the hot sun and cruelty in that cotton field, she thought this party would be the highlight of her days there. She refused to miss it because she was a white woman. That in itself sounded ridicules. The wagon stopped and the overseers pulled the women down leading them into the large building.

When she followed May Bee inside, instead of male slaves, Dawn discovered white men smoking, talking, drinking and eating. They had been there a while from their drunken conversations and laughter. Her eyes widened. She estimated about fifty white men, including the plantation owner, seated behind decorated tables dressed in suits. Each looked the picture of wealth. On the tables in front of them sat gallon jugs and large glasses filled with brown liquor. Food of every description was displayed on serving trays for the men to choose from. Dawn watched them pull meat from the trays using little etiquette.

She glanced over the large room, shocked to see that around the walls stood opened ended troughs that must have been placed there after they left the previous evening.

Before Dawn's imagination got the best of her, May Bee and the other females were directed over to them. She followed May Bee who walked over and stood in front of a trough. The overseers she recognized and about ten other white men ordered the women to undress. They quickly removed their sack dresses. Her mouth agape, Dawn looked stunned as the overseers nudged the women down into the troughs. All conversations and laughter ceased as the plantation owner and his guests gazed with open mouths at the naked females.

To Dawn's expanding horror, straps were tied around each woman's hands and feet, their naked bodies exposed to all viewers. Dawn felt as if she would pass out when naked slave males were herded in and began to mount the women. She doubled over in pain defensively clutching her own vagina as she felt the savage penetration of May Bee's body.

It seemed as if every organ inside of her would burst from the intense pain. Dawn's screams mixed with those of May Bee and the other females giving testimony to the torture that had attacked their bodies. Her sense of superior reality was shattered as she experienced May Bee's suffering. Nothing in her wildest imagination could have foretold the coming of this tragic event. Experiencing this unbelievable horror swept her into an alien nightmare.

At that moment it came to Dawn that Cherry, as well as the mistress, had been lied to about the intent of the mating party. May Bee knew what was coming. She just didn't have the words to explain it. It was a human breeding party. Dawn doubled over with May Bee's pain again and called out, "Meow!" The sound of water splashing alerted Dawn that the catfish had returned.

"Meow look at the brutal assaults on these women. There is no name in a civilized society to describe this savagery."

"Honey chile 'perencin' slavery sho' ain't nothing like readin' 'bout it, is it?"

114

"No wonder their descendants carry the weight of those crimes committed against their female ancestors to this day. How can we ever be forgiven?" she asked as she watched the brutal attacks taking place. "Meow this can't be real."

"Honey chile, I'm mighty 'fraid far might near three centuries dis was de life of de female slave. Matin' to produce babies dat become free labor for de plantation masters. She was how de owner replenished his lost property. Thay didn't tell ya in dem history books dat it was de female slave's body dat bore de sting of de worst abuse dat ever existed in dis country? Hur body served two races of men bearin' da births of both races all hur life. She slaved in cotton fields de same as de men as well as in de plantation homes. But de labor producin' business was whare hur body was most used."

"Oh no!"

"It come to be a labor machine to produce free labor as long as cotton was king. A machine oiled with da sperm of any male hur master gave his female slave to mate with. If hur master was lucky, she produced twenty births in hur lifetime. History of slave families torn apart was less common to de business of slavery. Dat plantation master needed dem births not to form families but so dat de babies

born could grow into good labor hands belonging only to him. Member de reason gave by de owner of de plantation for lettin go his overseer who killed de female baby slave. Dats why de slave woman begged not for da giver of da sperm but de babies dat come from his sperm, babies dat she cared for 'til thay was taken. A scar she carried to hur grave.

"Her descendants still carry those scars, Meow. You not only hear the bitterness in their voices but see it in eyes that look with hatred at what was done back then."

"If de slave master saw a male slave, he thought might make strong healthy babies from 'nother plantation, he paid for dat buck to mate with his female slave. Fathers of slave babies was neber welcomed to de wicked business of slavery."

Dawn watched Meow's lime green eyes roll around its head.

"It makes sense. Why would the master want a father involved? Oh, God. I never would have thought of it in those terms. What purpose would he serve?" Dawn sobbed as she watched one male release his sperm before another fell upon May Bee.

Milk suddenly flowed from May Bee's breasts. The male slave's lips covered one. May Bee uttered a cry begging him not to suck her; the milk was for her babies.

His lips slipped away from the breast. Dawn felt the pain of his intrusion as though it was her body being penetrated. She looked around the room at the other screaming female slaves. The young ones who had had no experience with any man made her think of Mindy—as young as some of those lying in the troughs. No father would ever want his daughter to witness this kind of *party.*

"Long after de importation of slavery was outlawed de female slave come to be de major source to supply southern labor. Without hur, slavery wouda ended within fifty yeers after it started. Ever time a new slave baby was born, de longer slavery lasted. De use of hur body supported dat system for centuries if de truth be tole."

"Are you telling me she was used as a *machine* making babies for men she didn't even know?"

"She was discouraged from bein' close to de male slave or hur babies dat could be taken and sold at any time. Hur fears come from not knowing how long hur babies would be with hur from de day thay was born. Not many of dem females mated with one male. Most given to mate whare no father could be known. Multiple mates made sure she'd bear a child dat belonged to no man 'cept hur master. How 'bout dat fer yer report, honey chile?"

Dawn listened to the catfish as she heard it splashing around in the water.

"As long as he had de female slave to increase his labor supply, de wealth and life style for de slave masters seemed endless. But like all wicked men seeking to fill de linings of thay pockets at de expense of another human life, he made one sad mistake."

"Meow, he made many mistakes. Which one are you speaking of?" Dawn felt the harsh sensations of another male copulating with May Bee and turned her head as though she believed the male slave lying on top of May Bee could see her as well.

"Thay was many mistakes, honey chile. One of de biggest was dat, instead of 'llowin' only de buck to have hur body, he like de dope pusher who began to use his own drugs, sexually used hur hisself thanking nothing of how he placed his own chilen inside hur body. Dem chilen carried his genes and would one day seek to be freed from men who had demselves waged war to gain thay own freedom once upon a forgotten time. Honey chile had thay known dat it was thare leisurely pleasures dat would reproduce themselves, thay would've refrained from dem pleasures and de African slave might still be working free for 'em to dis day."

118

Meow's assessment forced Dawn to reflect on the odd professor's assessment of the same theory. Now she understood why the plantation master told his wife the mating party was not for her *delicate* eyes. This sadistic horror shouldn't have been viewed by any human eyes; not even an animal should have been subjected to it.

"No!" Dawn screamed as the next slave mounted May Bee.

"Dis was in de 18th century when de white man ruled over ever'one who was not white and male, honey chile. Only he made up de rights and wrongs of life. His power in dem times now gives ya an idea of how life was lived under his rule in dat century."

"Well, I'm ashamed of him, his rule and of myself coming from that kind of history. Even though we white Americans are no longer like those Americans back then, we are their descendants; we must live with the shame of what happened back then."

"Ya done seen enough, I'll take ya on back now so ya can write dat report on de life of de female slave."

"What about May Bee, what will she think of my leaving when the worst is upon her?"

"Ya will fade from hur mind as a pleasant memory."

119

"What about my mind and memory, Meow?" She heard water splash and knew the catfish was allowing her to think about what it was she wanted. "I realize I'm no more than a sojourner in this place, but I can't leave her, not now. I must stay until the seventh day when I will then return with you. Even if I'm unable to help May Bee save her babies from being sold, I must try. Not only for myself, but also for the women of my race who have already fought and died and those who will one day be born to continue the fight to right the wrongs done in this world of men."

"Honey chile ain't I already done said ya won't be da same when ya return to dat classroom. May Bee has 'lowed ya to view hidden secrets unknown to most."

"I agree. Learning true history this way has changed me. I won't be the same. Living with May Bee has added something to my life. I don't ever want to forget her and her babies." Dawn could see that the unconscionable, sinister party had the plantation owner and his intoxicated guests so aroused, they began to caress their own sexual organs. Their lust filled eyes dazzled as they gazed at the brutal assaults they'd come to enjoy. May Bee's pain had Dawn sick to her stomach. She hated that there was nothing she could do to stop what was happening to her. After the fourth group of males left the room, Dawn stared in horror as a fifth group was herded in to straddle the naked women. She felt shame for her country's history that would one day be distorted by those forced to write it.

Dawn now wished for the cotton field and the heat of the hot sun as she, at last, understood what May Bee meant when she said the master wasn't so bad. It was the young bucks that gave her a tussle. The memory of her words hit Dawn hard. It was horrible enough feeling May Bee's pain, but she could hear the screams of the younger female slaves not yet physically ready for mating.

This horror caused Dawn to think of May Bee's baby girls. She now realized why the slave woman never talked to them. What could she tell them but of the brutal lives they were destined to live? After the last males finished with the bodies of the slave women, they were washed down with water that was thrown on them by the men who had herded them in. The plantation owner and his guests, now drunk and sexually aroused, began to straddle the women themselves. They seemed happy to get what was left.

Dawn realized why the baby Jesus had to come into this world by Immaculate Conception. The filth of what she was witnessing was too horrific even for the rawest mind. It seemed, however, an enjoyable way for the slave master and his guests to end their party of feasting and human mating.

CHAPTER NINE

DAY FIVE

Before daybreak Friday morning, Dawn sat in front of May Bee's shack reliving her time there. She had lived through the horrors of her stay and believed she would survive day four unscathed. Once the mating party ended, the overseers had the women redress in clothes that was now wet, stuffing the leftover food inside the aprons they wore. After being returned to their rows, Dawn followed May Bee to the old women's shack to retrieve her babies. What they discovered inside angered May Bee and increased Dawn's fears.

She and May Bee walked in on one of the slave women whipping May Bee's oldest baby's behind with a wet rag. She was a slave who usually worked in the field but the women had been excused from field work that day. Dawn couldn't believe her eyes. The baby lay across the woman's lap screaming. May Bee rushed over and snatched her baby from the slave woman.

"Don't ya whup mine," she shouted.

"Don't know why ya care, Massa says she go sell both dem nigger babies from ya anyhow lack she done dem otters come from de mast'r." Dawn's mouth stood ajar. She stared from the crying baby to May Bee, over at the woman and back again.

"Nah she ain't cause Dawn gonna help me keep 'em."

"What Dawn? Ain't no Dawn. Jus' yer ghost tis what it is. In yer crazy head ya been talkin to. Dem babies go be sold just like mine. I knows it," the slave woman insisted.

"If ya whup mine agin I'ma tellin mast'r ya being stealin' from him and ya be sold right long wit' em."

The room got quiet. Dawn saw a frightful look creep onto the faces of the six women in the shack. She remembered the overseer who was fired after May Bee revealed his evil deed to the plantation owner. All six women fell to the dirt floor at May Bee's feet with outstretched hands. Dawn trembled and her hands tightened around her arms.

"Don't wanta be sold no mor. I's too ole! Lard knows I is!" the slave woman beating May Bee's baby cried out as she shook her head back and forth. "I ain't neber go hit dat chile agin." The others shook their heads *no* along with her.

"If ya tell ole mast'r we all be sol' down the river," one of the other women said. Dawn looked around to see all the women in tears.

"Lardy be don't tell massa, he will sell us all I recken," begged another.

May Bee's threat had them all terrified.

"Well, ya bet not hit nar one of mine no mo'!" May Bee warned as she took her other baby into her arms. Dawn watched the slave women rise from the floor then turn away wiping tears from their eyes.

Once they returned to May Bee's shack, she put her babies down on the filled sack. May Bee looked sadly over at Dawn as she ate the food that had been shoved into her apron.

After a while, she took her babies in her arms and asked. "Is ya gonna help me keep my babies?" Dawn heard the doubt in May Bee's voice and knew she had to do something.

"Before it's time for me to return to the catfish May Bee you will be able to keep your babies." Tears rolled down May Bee's cheeks as a smile lit up her face.

Dawn shook her head wondering what on earth had prompted her to think she could understand what drove these women. Nothing that had happened to this woman mattered but her love for her babies. All the women living on this plantation as slaves loved the babies they birthed.

Her thoughts turned to her own society. To take a woman's baby to sell would be a crime punishable by imprisonment. Who fathered the baby, would be the man the woman chose to impregnate her. The decision to have a child, in most cases, would be a consensual agreement. Dawn reflected that it would be unthinkable to take someone's child and sell it without being charged with kidnapping.

Yet, she knew, none of these laws applied in this society. The slave women had no rights, not even to their own lives. In their world, all that mattered to them were the babies who came from their bodies. The mistress was wrong about the slave women not knowing anything about love. They loved their babies. Those babies were all they had to love. When they were taken, a part of them died inside. Just as the mistress grieved her babies, they grieved theirs, too. They were no different from her, except for race.

Dawn lay down that night with her mind riveting from the horrifying party. She didn't mention it to May Bee.

126

Chills iced her spine when she remembered the horrors she had witnessed. May Bee had experienced the pain. She had only shared the feelings of that horrible pain.

Nightmares ravaged Dawn's dreams. She stood out in the cotton field; the heat of the sun beamed down on her face. Looking around, she wondered where everyone had gone. Her arms had begun to tan, causing her halter to deflect her skin. The blue shorts she wore hugged her white legs that had also begun to darken. Troughs, like those May Bee and the other female slaves were forced to lie in, stood scattered all around in the cotton field. Dawn saw so many she thought of them as coffins.

The scene scared her when she turned and saw naked white and black men running towards her. Dawn began to run, her heart pounding. When she turned to see how close they were upon her, she tripped and fell into one of the troughs. The naked men crowded around her. Hot blood rushed to her face. She struggled to keep from being smothered to death. Just as she was about to take her last breath the dream changed, and Dawn found herself standing beside May Bee and her babies at the river bank.

They waited for Meow to come for her. She looked up and down the river, anxious for the catfish's arrival. Dawn wanted to get back to her own century as quickly as possible before she found herself in another one of those awful troughs. This was not her century and she didn't want to become a part of it or its horrors.

The sound of dogs barking caused the two women to stare at each other in terror.

"Slave hunters come brang dogs to git May Bee and hur babies." May Bee screamed as she took off running. Down the river bank, May Bee ran with Dawn beside her. Through weeds and over sticks, they ran as sharp brush cut into May Bee's legs drawing blood. Dawn felt the pain of the sharp brush that cut into May Bee's legs, but she kept running. The faster she ran the louder the snarls of the hounds grew. The babies cried as May Bee and Dawn leaped over two large logs in their path. Neither woman stopped until the thick lips and vicious teeth of the hounds had them cornered.

The hounds pulled against their leashes. Saliva poured from their jowls as the red hair on their backs gleamed wet with sweat. There the mistress stood, holding the leashes of her three blood hounds in one hand, her cattail whip in the other. She, like the hounds, breathed deeply as though exhausted by the chase.

"I got your ass now wench. My hounds will eat you for dinner." A satanic glare marred her features as the

mistress let the hounds loose on May Bee. Her babies in her arms, May Bee turned and jumped free-falling into the river. Dawn jumped in behind her as she screamed for Meow to come save her.

Dawn heard her own screams as she felt herself being shaken awake. Shivering, she realized May Bee had awakened her from the nightmare. Her sobs came out in a rush mingling with those of the babies.

"Yesdidy done got to ya. Shouldn't gone dar no how. May Bee take ya back to de river and dat catfish."

Thank God! It was only a dream, Dawn thought shivering as she clung to May Bee still sobbing.

She cried so hard May Bee stroked her back trying to console her.

"Let's go 'fo it's time to go pickin."

"May Bee I can't allow you to take me back to the river." Dawn's body trembled as she breathed in and out to calm herself. "Suppose someone saw you going there before Sunday?"

"It be alright Dawn. May Bee ain't gonna let ya be hurt."

Dawn felt shame having May Bee protect her when she knew it was May Bee who needed protecting. The nightmare had her so shaken, getting out of there had been the only thing on her mind. May Bee's offer to take her back made her think of the mistress and her hounds, and what might result if she took her back before Sunday.

"No, May Bee, they'd have those hounds come after you. If you are caught, you'd get beaten and whipped if not worse. There is no doubt in my mind you would never see your babies again. Thanks, but no thanks."

"Dawn," May Bee started to argue.

"No, May Bee! You have no one to fend for you as it is, not even the slave men can help you. Without your desire to find a little bit of love, what a sad life it would be even for those you struggle to keep." Dawn couldn't help but think of the old slave woman who had all her children sold over time. Even the old woman's feeble daughter by the master and her daughter's daughter the Mistress had given away once she discovered her husband had fathered them both. She carried that grief in her heart as though they had died. Dawn reached over and hugged May Bee. She was so glad it was only an awful nightmare and that May Bee and her babies were safe. There was no way she could place her life in that kind of danger.

Dawn sat outside working to calm herself. Oh God, how she had believed the mating party would give her something to report back that would render some semblance of sanity in this insane society. It wasn't to be. Dawn knew that while the day's travesties stained her heart, it was the nightmares that had finally driven the reality of the female slave's crippling life home for her. The personal attack on her when she dreamt of falling into the trough created a fear she had never experienced in her life. Being hunted by someone with the right to take your life, though a dream, brought May Bee's paralyzing existence crashing down on Dawn's former beliefs of America history.

She had been dumped into a century where black women and their children lived in horrors worse than working as slaves. In her century, what happened the day before would have been considered an atrocity. Here, every day of the slave woman's life was filled with atrocities. Only when white women were assaulted by men other than their husbands was it a crime. For the slave woman, it was an accepted way of life. If she hadn't forgotten her cell phone, she would have blown social media up with atrocities that would shock the world.

Dawn listened to the splash of water as Meow beat his tail against the waves of whatever river it swam. She wondered how he knew of her troubles when she hadn't called for him?

"It come to me dat dis life might become a bit frightful for yer delicate mind. Meow kin git ya back in a hurry." Dawn thought about what the catfish was telling her it would do for her. She shook her head.

"No Meow. I've come too far and stayed too long to abandon what you brought me here to do. Like it or not, it is my destiny to see this through to the end. There must be a reason I'm here."

"Honey chile might be a bit 'f truth in dat. Meow is what ya folks would call an alien space traveler. Otters like Meow travel de roadways of de sky moving in and out of worlds de same as we move in and out of yers. Meow has discovered many untold secrets inside yer whirling rivers.

Dawn knew discoveries were always turning up in the earth's oceans, but she never thought of rivers hiding secrets.

"Decided it best to become one of yer river catfish till I found who knows how to win de game of life. My moves through de rivers leaves no trail to follow."

Dawn understood the problems an alien would have trying to be human in her world.

"Traveling through de river as a big ol' blue catfish, I ain't got no fight wit dat slender gray channel catfish and

I don't even mind dat flat head cat. As I pass de black cat we smile and go our separate ways."

Dawn knew it would be much different if he attempted to be human.

"De catfish come in all sizes and colors wit different looks and nobody cares down in dese waters. Too much being tossed into de rivers by yer kind. My being big and blue don't bother de cats dats long and skinny. Don't no other catfish care if ya black, blue, green or gray. Even brown is allowed. When Meow done seed enough of dis tragic world, I will move on to otter worlds and see if thay understand de rules and how de game of life is won."

Dawn wondered what game he was speaking of. "You brought me here to help me learn the truths of my country's history. Now that I am here, I'm going to learn them. I know I can't change history, but I am responsible for not taking the time to learn it.

"I was swimmin 'round lookin for someone dat needed ta learn how ta win de game of life. I saw ya thare on de bank thanking 'bout how to give a report dat would out do dat classmate of yers. It come to me dat I could take ya far into de future if ya wanted to learn more, but it was de past ya needed to know. I know'd I kinda scared ya but yer curiosity got de best of ya. Know'd it would be a hard life ya

would visit but ya was willin and I was able, so we took off. When I spit ya out on da river bank ya looked de same as May Bee, scared 'bout to death, but ya stayed after all. Made me proud, honey chile."

"Meow I'm anything but proud of myself. That nightmare seemed so real. It was no longer only May Bee's fear but my own fear I felt. When I fell into that trough and couldn't get out, I shut my eyes horrified of what those men would do to me." Dawn heard the splash of water and knew that catfish was probably responsible for her experiencing that dream.

"I can still smell the awful sweat of those bloodhounds. My skin burned thinking any minute they would attack May Bee, the babies and me." Dawn again heard the water splash.

"More dan happy to take ya on back."

"It's only one more day Meow."

Anyway, Dawn thought, t*here were too many terrible things she already witnessed not to know it's only going to get worse.*

"Honey chile, what if it's only a game of slave and master brought to be by de unknown? Who knows who shall win in de end, de slave or de master?" The water splashed

and Dawn knew the catfish had added another dimension to this wild adventure.

"Ya now know de life of de female slave. Yer journey's end is to find a way to help May Bee keep hur babies, adder all, it's hur love of dem babies dat certainly d'clares hur humanity. See ya Sunday. Be thare early. Ya got a report to do fo' yer classmates 'member."

CHAPTER TEN

DAY SIX

Whare is God when ya need Him? May Bee thought that Saturday morning as she listened to the sound of the overseer's horse hooves walk through the cotton field. Their whips could be heard from afar. When someone screamed, she didn't look up or around. Her eyes stayed fixed on the cotton she picked. May Bee knew she could easily become their next victim.

Her mind traveled back to what Dawn told her she must do in order to keep her babies.

"May Bee, you must give your baby girls to the mistress in order to keep them." Her mouth had dropped open. Dawn wanted her to give her babies to her evil mistress. She had believed Dawn to be a good ghost brought to her by that catfish to help her keep her babies. Now it all came out.

"Nah Dawn, May Bee ain't go gave hur babies to dat witch." Witch was the name May Bee had heard Dawn call the mistress on many occasions. She knew the witch would beat her to death if she did what Dawn said. As she watched the overseers ride by Dawn, May Bee wondered what they would do if they could see that white woman out there in that cotton field with so little clothes on standing next to slave men? What would the mistress say if she could see Dawn wander around her plantation home like it was her own home?

May Bee couldn't quite understand the white woman ghost who had come to help her keep her babies. She was so afraid the master would find Dawn lying next to her and her babies those first nights that she couldn't sleep. She lay on her corn shuck bed trembling as she waited for something awful to happen to her. She imagined a horrible fate after being forced to explain the white woman's presence. When May Bee realized that her master couldn't see Dawn her fears subsided, and she was glad the catfish had brought her. She had become like her friend the tree; someone she could talk to and not worry about what she said getting back to the people who owned her.

After the first few days, Dawn rose when she rose and helped her get her babies ready to take to the slave women's shack. It amazed her to see Dawn out in that hot cotton field picking cotton with her and the rest of the slaves;

cotton she made sure no one could see her put in her sack. When the overseer stomped that baby to death, she watched in horror as Dawn picked up a stick and hit him. She thanked God he never felt the licks from the stick; she surely couldn't have helped Dawn.

Dawn didn't act like any white woman or man she'd ever encountered. At that moment a warmth began to stir in her heart for her ghost visitor. It took a while for May Bee to get used to her ways. The white woman talked all the time and asked so many questions about everything, especially about the people who owned her and why they did the things they did. It was kind of interesting that what they did bothered Dawn more than it bothered her. She had to live in that life all the time. May Bee didn't understand most things she was telling her, but she liked to watch Dawn play with her babies.

May Bee never welcomed the master in her bed, but Dawn hated when he came. She talked about him something terrible which made May Bee laugh, something she had never been able to do before she came. There were things about her master and the mistress she thought but could never put into words the way her ghost did. As strangely as Dawn appeared, May Bee had grown to like the ghost. Most of all she loved to lay on her sack bed and listen to Dawn tell her about the things from her own time; a time where women her color kept their babies without fear of them ever being taken. Where women like her could pick their own man to love. She said they owned themselves and no master could make them work till they dropped dead. What a life. May Bee hoped to go there once she died and left her miserable existence on the plantation behind. If she ever found her babies that the mistress sold it would be like ending up in heaven.

May Bee didn't understand what Dawn wanted her to do, but she did know the mistress would not be pleased. She'd sold her children and many other slave women's children. Even the old slave woman, Mammie, May Bee lived with as a child had all the babies, she conceived on the plantation sold by the mistress. Her eyes filled with tears when she had to leave Mammie after the master had her shack built so he could have his time with her.

May Bee knew the mistress couldn't stop her husband from visiting the slave women's shacks, but the slave women lived at the mercy of the mistress. An eerie look gathered in the mistress's eyes each time a slave woman gave birth to a baby believed to be fathered by her husband.

The slave woman would beg on her knees to be allowed to keep her baby. The demonic gleam in her eyes lit up as she let the slave woman hold the baby one last time before the buyers rode off with their new property. What Dawn wanted her to do would surely cause her to lose her babies forever.

May Bee became nervous when Dawn walked over and asked if she remembered their conversation from the night before?

She didn't want to think about their conversation. She continued to pick the cotton in front of her as they stared at slave hunters cross the cotton field pulling two run-away slaves by the yokes tied around their necks; one male slave and the other a pregnant female. May Bee's body froze when her eyes fell on the deep bloody gashes on their legs from the teeth of the bloodhounds that walked beside them.

May Bee looked down to see Dawn rub her leg and noticed that they were now as brown as her babies. *Dawn's thoughts must be on the bad dream she'd had the night before,* May Bee thought. Each looked at the other. Those two slaves reminded May Bee of what Dawn told her happened in her dream.

May Bee's mind turned to the first day she sat against her friend, the tree, and watched Dawn pop out of the catfish's mouth. It all seemed so strange, the same as when the shaman found her lost and cold after she wandered away from her village. He had brought her back to her parents telling them she had been living with spirits. He said that she could see things no one else could see and one day she would leave the village never to return.

Not long after that she and her mother sat by the river's edge when men with spears came and took them away to live among the white ones who made slaves of them. So many unusual things had taken place in her life that when that catfish spit Dawn out of its mouth it became just another unexplainable event in May Bee's life.

May Bee couldn't figure out how Dawn thought she could help her keep her babies. All the white women in her life hated the slaves they owned. She was like no other white person May Bee had ever met but even she, May Bee knew was no match for her mistress.

Tears seeped from May Bee's eyes as she remembered how she got down on her knees and begged the mistress not to sell her first baby everyone said looked just like the master. The mistress sold him anyway. When the second baby was born the mistress came down with a buyer just after his birth and pulled him from her breast. That one looked just like the first one, she told Dawn. The mistress said she was selling them because May Bee caused her to miscarry. How could that be? May Bee wasn't even on the plantation during the mistress's pregnancies.

Dawn didn't understand when the mistress made up her mind about something, neither slaves on the plantation nor the judge could change it. The more you begged her for something the more determined she was not going to give it to you.

When Dawn shared with May Bee what she must do if she wanted to keep her babies, it was something May Bee couldn't understand and surely something she was afraid to do. Dawn said it was the only way.

She told May Bee that she must tell the mistress she should not cook the chicken but the duck she knew the master enjoyed. May Bee didn't want to do what she asked her to do but Dawn insisted. Of course, the mistress threatened that if May Bee didn't cook the chicken, she would beat her unmercifully.

After they left that evening, Dawn told May Bee she must tell the driver to wait for her to get her babies and take them back to the plantation house. Scared to death the driver wanted to know why he had to take her back.

"My ghost, Dawn, said so." she answered looking at him with tears flooding her cheeks. "It's my ghost." The slave turned around to take her and her babies to the plantation house watching her oddly the whole way. Dawn continued to drill May Bee as to what she must tell the mistress.

When they arrived, Dawn stood so close by May Bee she could feel her trembling. The house female slave opened the back door after May Bee knocked several times looking shocked to find May Bee standing there with her babies.

May Bee shook so hard, Dawn screamed, "May Bee if you don't do as I say that big old fat catfish will swallow you and your babies just like he swallowed me!" May Bee stuttered but finally got out that she wanted to see the mistress. The slave woman hurried away and soon returned with the mistress. She stood in a long brown housedress with a black shawl wrapped tightly around her shoulders; her brown hair was partly covered with a hair net. The ends of her hair hung out of the net. She stared with wide blue eyes at May Bee.

"Do it now, May Bee. Now!" Dawn screamed in her ear.

May Bee rushed inside and tossed the babies into the mistress's arms crying, "Sell des babies, I don't wanna neber see 'em no mo. Take 'em. Da yers to hev' cause I don't wanna 'em sickly babies wit me no mo!"

144

May Bee turned to walk out the door; the babies began to scream and kick to get free from the mistress's arms. Quick as a flash, the mistress tossed the babies to the house slave like rag dolls and reached for her long cattail whip. She caught May Bee before she reached the door and struck her repeatedly.

Dawn felt the licks and screamed as loudly as May Bee.

"What you mean you don't want 'em you had 'em didn't you?" the mistress screamed beating and thrashing May Bee until she fell to the floor.

Dawn bent and twisted her back as she shielded her face to keep it from being hit; maneuvers that didn't help May Bee. The mistress struck her everywhere she could land a lick as May Bee rolled back and forth across the floor.

"They yours and you going to keep them, you hear me? They ain't going nowhere but with you, wench. Done laid down and had these messes now you go give me these sickly babies ain't nobody go want."

For a minute, Dawn believed the mistress would kill them both. Though no one heard her screams except May Bee and her babies, Dawn prayed the mistress would soon grow tired. She hated that she had caused May Bee to get such a beating. It hadn't been a part of her plan.

"Give them to that wench!" the mistress yelled as she struggled to catch her breath. "She will care for her own sick messes."

With that, she gave May Bee several more licks as May Bee took her screaming babies from the house slave.

"Telling me what you ain't go do is exactly what you will do. You go keep those sickly babies long as you and they live, black wench!"

There are some ways that never change. True to form, Dawn knew she had trapped the mistress as though she was a criminal seated in court.

The driver helped May Bee struggle aboard the wagon as the mistress ran outside waving her cattail screaming that May Bee will keep those tainted, sickly babies forever.

"Oh, May Bee, I am so sorry I got you a beating," Dawn cried still feeling the pain of the cattails as they drove off. "I never intended for that to happen." She looked over her own body to see if any cattail marks covered it as they did May Bee's. Finding none she gave a sigh of relief.

"I am so sorry." Dawn continued to apologize as she thought back to how the mistress had beaten the slave woman who told her she didn't want the wool scarf she was accused of stealing. The mistress had made her wear it every day. She had forgotten about the beating the slave woman endured. Dawn looked over at May Bee who held tightly to her babies aware that there was no other way to outsmart the mistress. Even if the mistress wanted to, she could never accept May Bee's babies. She would be the disgrace of her white society caring for babies born from the body of a slave.

"Whare's God when ya need 'em? Dat God is ever whare. I done got to keep my babies, dat's all I care. He brung ya hare to give May Bee a lit' bit 'f love." Her swollen lips spread into a smile that Dawn hadn't expected. Tears flowed down her cheeks.

As soon as they arrived at May Bee's row of shacks the male slave jumped from the wagon and took off running. As he raced down the shack rows, his shouts caused all the slaves to gather to hear him bellow that May Bee got to keep her babies. He had heard the mistress say they would be sold before. Now, he was telling the new story of how the mistress said May Bee *had* to keep her babies. He'd heard with his own ears and informed them of the beating she received for even suggesting that the mistress sell them.

May Bee was helped from the wagon by the women in her row of shacks. They administered care to her wounds while they smiled and talked about the latest event in May Bee's life. Dawn could feel the happiness in the air as the

147

women placed more food in the large pot outside in celebration. The fire under it created light as evening darkened the day.

Before long an old female slave supported by two sticks and an old male slave approached May Bee who sat nursing her babies. May Bee's eyes widened as did Dawn's.

"Tell me dat ole devil says ya gits to keep yers thare," the old slave woman said pointing to May Bee's nursing babies.

"Yesum, Mammie. Mistress lettin' me keep 'em."

Dawn stared at the old slave woman May Bee had told her so much about. She remembered her name. May Bee had shared with her that the mistress had sold all of Mammie's children plus the ones she gave away. Dawn envisioned the old slave woman running with her babies to keep them from being sold from her before being sold to the judge's plantation. What a horrible life to live.

"How dat be?" Mammie asked as she allowed the male slave to help her lower her thin body to the ground in front of May Bee.

"It were Dawn help me keep 'ems Mammie." Dawn placed her hand on May Bee's arm. She knew they couldn't see her.

"Its hur ghost done it Mammie. She sho' got one!" the slave woman she threatened to tell on after seeing her whip her baby shouted. "Heerd May Bee talkin' to hur out in dat field jus yesdiddy when she picked cotton for hur."

"Picked cotton for hur? What dis ghost look to be, gal?" Mammie's eyes never left May Bee's.

"Color like de gurls come ta de see de mistress Mammie. Hur hair jess likes de sun and eyes dat look like dat sky when ain't no clouds and de sun is up." Dawn squeezed May Bee's arm as she moved closer to her.

"Ain't no ghost dar lookin' like dem gurls come see dat mistress gon' stop dat evil devil from selling niggers' chilen May Bee." Mammie's eyes stared hard into May Bee's. A sudden loud voice caused everyone to stare upward.

"Mammie, May Bee is a mother who loves her babies and wants to keep them just like you wanted to keep yours. She's no nigger. You're no nigger." Dawn looked with the others to see seated in the night sky what looked to be an old man with long white hair hanging in empty space. There was so much hair on and around his face you couldn't see it; just white hair flowing in the night air. Dawn recognized the sound of Meow's voice coming from all that hair. She

149

wondered what had become of him and why his words sounded so different.

"Mammie you were a good mother to all the children born to you." His hair moved outward as if a hand had brushed it aside.

Dawn saw tears wet the slave woman's face at the mention of her babies she lost.

"One day slavery will end, and the slave mothers will be able to keep their babies just like white mothers." Sounds of shock traveled through the crowd of slaves seated on the ground; their mouths opened as they continued to stare up into the sky at the strange sight.

"Will it end for us, ya thank?" asked a young male slave who stood looking up.

"Slave men will one day fight for their freedom and win. They will no longer work as slaves but will be paid for the work they do the same as white men. They will have families that cannot be taken from them." A breeze swept across the night air as the strange sight above their heads disappeared causing the crowd to gasp in wonder. Shouts of joy and pain rang out as the slaves sang together:

"Go down Moses, way down in Egypt's land. Tell ol' Pharaoh to let my people go."

The hairs on Dawn's arms tingled as she listened to the pain in their voices, they sang different songs. She stared at the big blue catfish that gazed down at them from above, a site only she could see. Their voices vibrated through the night air like waves of a rushing stream. Dawn's heart stirred as stars and the moon lit up the night sky surrounding Meow. Dawn felt her own euphoria; knowing that freedom for the slaves would surely come.

CHAPTER ELEVEN

DAY SEVEN

There were no calendars or clocks available to them but somehow all the slaves knew it was Sunday. She could hear their movements as they walked slowly past May Bee's shack down the path to where they would meet with the slave preacher the plantation owner allowed to preach to them. Dawn rose still feeling the euphoria from the night before. May Bee hurried as she and Dawn dressed her babies. They left the shack and walked straight into the woods retracing their steps to the tree and the river where they hoped to find the catfish waiting.

There were no signs of the catfish when they first arrived. Dawn walked with May Bee over to the tree where Dawn first saw her seven days before. Overcome with sadness, they turned to face each other as tears rolled down their cheeks. The babies reached for Dawn. She took them.

"May Bee if there was any way I could take you and these babies back with me I would." Her tears were coming so fast she could hardly see.

"Ya good woman Dawn, when ya go back to yer world tell 'em 'bout how bad it is in the slave's world and for de slave woman ya must tell 'em not to forget 'bout us. Dat we hope better will come by and by."

Dawn's heart saddened; it would come but too late for May Bee and her babies.

"I will May Bee. I promise. I will tell them in my report I told you about."

"When ya come agin May Bee won't let no harm come to ya."

May Bee sat down against her friend, the tree. Dawn placed May Bee's babies in her arms and was about to let her know she probably would never return when a large wave appeared so unexpectedly it splashed water over Dawn, May Bee, and the babies. Meow's wide mouth opened as the catfish landed on the bank spitting out more water. Its green eyes rolled around in its head as if looking for them. Seeing the catfish, Dawn hugged May Bee and kissed each baby. She blinked and in less than the time it took to take another breath, she found herself back in her own time standing next to the red handle of the locked hatch. She waved goodbye to the huge tail of the blue catfish.

****

"She has not been to class since the class challenged us last week to do the oral report today. She's probably a no-show," Dawn heard Tony say as she hurried into the classroom. Tony, Shirley and Tina usually sat in the last row; today they sat in front. Tony, the most verbal of the three, sat with his long legs crossed waiting with the rest of the students.

Dawn pulled her blonde hair behind her head taking in a deep breath. She handed the instructor her written report as she stood before the class to deliver the oral version. Smiling at her from the back of the classroom a female student said,

"Hey, Miss Perry Mason, I haven't seen or heard from you all week. Did you take a vacation? You look as though you have been somewhere tanning."

"Or at least on the beach lying in the sun all week," a white male student commented. He smiled and Dawn smiled back.

Tony, who sat beside Shirley, restlessly crossed, and uncrossed his legs waiting to hear what she had to say. Dawn noticed how Shirley glared at her with a look that dared her to try and force them to believe history about their female ancestors they felt untrue. Beside her sat Tina who rolled her eyes and looked off as if she knew what was coming.

Dawn knew the other fourteen students also anxiously waited to hear what her oral report contained.

In her mind's eye, Dawn saw herself running beside May Bee and her babies trying to escape the vicious hounds pursuing them. She trembled as she remembered the fear she felt. But it was seeing the catfish appear in the sky the night before that disturbed her the most. She asked herself *if it was as Meow stated, all a game played by unseen forces with even the slave masters as pawns, why was so horrible a game played with human lives? Worse, what if it's still being played? If the game is not yet over who will win in the end? Would she return? If so for what reason? Her classmates had no clue how far this country had evolved since the days of slavery. Who, she wondered was really in control? It reminded her of Greek Mythology and their gods*

As bad as slavery might seem to them, Dawn knew Tony, Shirley and Tina had no understanding of the depth of horrors slaves endured. As she now stood in her own century, Dawn was aware that a new and different era was already evolving. She wondered what that evolutionary change would be like for those yet to be born.

"There is no such history as Black history in our country," Dawn's voice rang out loudly and clearly as she stared at her classmates and the instructor who sat in the audience with the students.

"Everything that has occurred in this country is every American's history— good and bad." Her fingers trembled but she knew her report had to be given.

"It is about us as a people and the choices and decisions made by our ancestors hundreds of years ago. Those choices and decisions have brought us to the present day. My report speaks of one aspect of that history, the life of the American female slave."

Dawn took in a deep breath and continued, "My research led me to a time in history I had no understanding of. It isn't that I didn't know this period in history happened, but now realize why it is history we as white Americans no longer want to discuss. My findings mandated that I ask one of the most disturbing questions of history." Looking at her classmates Dawn took another deep breath and asked,

"How much mind altering did it take to convince an entire nation of people that building our country through the suffering, mutilation, rape and enslavement of other humans was their Christian duty? I say nation because the North is just as much a part of this history as the South. A tragic history that as a white American, I must revisit centuries later. Had it not been for my thorough research, one could

157

never have made me believe slavery for the slave woman could have possibly been that horrific. Her life was the worst in the history of our nation for any woman to endure; she endured it for nearly three hundred years. In the cotton fields, she toiled while carrying babies soon to be born."

'Ya can't tell 'em dat babies was trampled to death they won't b'lieve it to be true."

Dawn shivered envisioning the hoof of the overseer's horse trampling the baby to death.

"Treated worse than if she were an animal, work for this female started before daybreak. In fields and in plantation houses she slaved only to return to her shack unable to sufficiently feed herself or her children."

Dawn realized she couldn't tell them about the food the mistress had her starving slave women throw to the dogs. They wouldn't want to believe that either. How could she have known? She wouldn't have believed it possible had she not seen it with her own eyes.

"While it is true some female slaves lived inside the master's house, even those slaves could be summoned at any time for any reason. Their duties had to be fulfilled day or night; just as if they were working in the fields. Their lives, just as those in the field, belonged to their masters. Though their work differed, the treatment they received played out the same. No woman in this room can imagine giving birth to babies owned by someone else, babies that could be sold at any time for any reason. The slave woman's most important job was having children owned by only her master. Her womb was oiled with the sperm of any slave or white male, her body was mated with. She was sexually exploited by many races of men for nearly three centuries. It is American history; a way of life drawn up for the slave woman through no fault of her own." Dawn stopped and took another deep breath. Her eyes became teary as she remembered the trauma of the mating party and its cruel purpose.

Had it not been for Meow, Dawn was destined to live oblivious to that part of American history. The telling of it brought the horrors back fresh in her mind. Tears filled her eyes—she needed to hurry and finish.

"The female slave became the means by which the slave masters replenished their labor force. Her body was used to give birth for anyone who owned her, sometimes being sold seven or eight times before her death. If her master or mistress were *lucky*, many of their slave women produced twenty or more babies in their lifetime, most sold away from them"

Dawn paused as gasps could be heard throughout the classroom. She knew those students could never have endured any of what she witnessed.

"The slave *family* concept was not real because a slave could be sold at any time. Slave fathers' ability to protect their families was for the most part unheard of. Like with any of the slave master's animals the male had no say in the births he was responsible for.

"That's the truth," Tina said then covered her mouth as if surprised she could be heard.

"Slave owners had no need for real families, or slave fathers because all slaves belonged to them. Most mating of the females took place with multiple males so that no father could be known. Even when the pregnancy resulted from the master's mating with the females, those babies were sold the same as the rest. No difference was made between the slave master's children and the children by the slave male. If the slave master or his mistress chose to sell a slave, black or white, they were sold."

Dawn watched Tony uncross his legs as he rubbed the back of his fair hand reminding Dawn that he also carried the gene of an unknown white male, the same as May Bee's babies, and many other slaves she had seen on the judge's plantation. The white color was all the people of that day

160

thought was passed to the offspring. No one realized that the genes of the master also made up those babies. He unknowingly was reproducing himself.

"The slave woman gave birth not knowing how long her children would be with her before they were sold; children she begged to be allowed to keep."

Dawn thought of the mistress's benediction for May Bee's babies. Her head bent toward the ground, "she moved through life having no idea when her circumstances would suddenly change, and she might find herself sold to a new master; her body used by different mates in her new slave environment."

Dawn understood why May Bee never talked to her babies. Why would she?

"The horrors of her life began as soon as she was thought to be old enough to work and ended when death took her out of her miserable existence." *That would not be something a mother would want to tell her daughters.*

"Whoa! Your research is thorough sister girl," Shirley said raising her hand to cover her mouth.

"She was born in this country with no understanding of what race meant, or why it sealed her fate to live the life of a slave until her death."

Dawn stared at the students hearing Mindy's voice, *"my Toby is no different than me."*

It was the same way she learned to see May Bee. A woman living a different life but with the same pain, happiness, sadness, and most of all love; no different than her own emotions.

"No female on this earth should have had to endure those conditions, yet it is our nation's history; a history that should never be forgotten or repeated on this planet."

Startled faces gazed at her. Dawn looked beyond her classmates as May Bee's life flooded her thoughts. She remembered she and May Bee pushing rags in between the cracks in the walls to keep the rain from pouring in on them. They ended up squeezed together in a corner of May Bee's shack where the roof was solid, hoping to keep the two babies dry. Waking up half asleep, the two had taken the babies to the old women's shack and headed out to the fields where cotton waited to be picked.

"There is always a power beyond human depravity," Dawn said as she stared at her audience. "God, in his mercy, graced the slave woman with love for the children who came and went from her body, her arms, and soon her life. For her children, she lived colorblind loving them no matter what color or condition they came to her. She held that little bit of love under her breasts; a love that burned in her heart long after they were sold. It was a love that could not be destroyed even though many times it came to her whitewashed."

Dawn took a deep breath as she remembered May Bee's last words the night before sleep overtook them both.

'Tell 'em, Dawn, how it was for de slave woman in hur life. Tell 'em so de don't forgit 'bout us.' Both their tears had fallen as Dawn wrapped her arms around May Bee.

"It is our country's history," she said. "A history where American women existed in skeletal bodies producing babies to ensure the survival of free labor for this nation."

Her mind inside May Bee's world, Dawn said to her classmates, "There has never been, to my knowledge, any psychological studies on the generational tremors of the female slave. Who knows or understands the damage done to her and her offspring because of those atrocities endured during that time in American history?"

The students and the instructor sat with open mouths.

"What we do know is that to this day her descendants still carry those scars. That is why it is impossible to equate the conditions of immigrant people from other countries with the descendants of the African slaves brought to this country.

The Africans who sold other Africans from the continent of Africa have no idea how they destroyed those lives."

She saw the African exchange students look at each other and shake their heads.

"After being taken as slaves, I believe, all that was needed was a little kindness to get what their owners desired from them. Instead, my research led me to a history of brutal force and racial breeding used to gain our nation's wealth. The slave masters destroyed what the slaves could have become for them and corrupted the very principles our nation put in place after the Revolutionary War."

Dawn gazed into faces that held looks of shock.

"There was nothing humane, as I once believed, about the treatment of the slave woman during that time in our history. As a result, the legacy of Democracy we offer the rest of the world has always been compromised. Even the Civil War, which was said to have freed the slaves, was never fought for that purpose. In truth, it was fought to determine whether the North or the South would control this nation."

To her surprise, neither Tony, Shirley nor Tina said a word to discredit her report, yet their mouths stood ajar as Dawn continued uninterrupted.

"After the Civil War, we failed to keep our promises to those still under our power not caring that they gave their lives to help us win that war. As a newly freed person, I too would have struggled to understand what freedom meant for me. The nation's failure to keep promises made to those freed people created a history as bizarre as that troubled system many fought to end. For another hundred years, we used the tyranny of Jim Crow Laws to continue the destruction of the former slave woman's life, allowing white men to enter her home and sexually violate her—even with a husband, father or other male relative living in the home. No different than her slave life. Few, if any, Americans want to remember that time in history, but it is American history. Our ancestors' decisions and actions caused that history. I don't believe, even to this day, we have figured out where they went wrong or how to right those wrongs. For that reason, it is part of our American history we are now living to regret."

Dawn stared beyond the students who looked at her dumbfounded as she moved to leave the podium.

Tony stood up, gave his written report to the instructor, and walked over taking Dawn's hands, "I have nothing to add based on what you have just shared Miss

Perry Mason." He kissed her cheek and walked out of the classroom.

A vision of the plantation cotton fields suddenly appeared before her. In it, Dawn saw thousands of white statues. The air she breathed burned her throat. Blood ran through the fields and in the air. When Dawn came to herself, she sucked in her breath as she looked up at the instructor wondering, *what on earth had happened in that cotton field?*

"Are you alright?" the instructor asked placing his hand on her shoulder.

"Yes," she said seeing that everyone else had left the classroom.

"That was an astounding report you gave Dawn. I can't believe you accomplished it in just a week," he said reviewing her documented sources and references.

She smiled, thanked him, and left the room.

****

Dawn hurried down the hallway. Something must have happened on the plantation. She wondered what it meant for May Bee and her babies. She needed to find out. Her throat felt dry. Walking into the cafeteria, Dawn went to the water fountain, got a cup of ice water, and took a seat still troubled by the scene in the cotton field. The ice water tasted refreshing. In May Bee's world fresh water was priceless.

In seven days, her life had completely changed. All her former beliefs shattered. May Bee's life consumed her thoughts. Whatever she had once believed, she knew better now. Her previous understanding of life for the female slaves had been whitewashed. She could still feel the raw penetration of the mating day brutality that sickened her as it whirled through her mind.

It occurred to Dawn that she would have to face her friends. She knew they had expected her to blast the black students about the history of the female slave. No one, not even the instructor, had been prepared for her report. Tony had called her Miss Perry Mason. She had done a damn thorough job. They all knew it. She thought about Meow and smiled.

Voices behind her pulled her out of her thoughts. She soon realized they belonged to Shirley and Tina. Because of the partition that divided the cafeteria, they didn't know she sat on the other side listening to their conversation.

"That damn white girl shocked everyone in the class," she heard Tina say. "Told that report as if she was there herself. I couldn't believe what I was hearing."

"Did you see the looks on the faces of the rest of the class?" Shirley asked.

Tina chuckled. "They were just as shocked as we were, especially those African students. Even Tony had to sit and take notice. Her report was that thorough. Can you believe if it wasn't for that Civil War, we might still be pushing out free labor?"

"Isn't that the truth," Shirley replied laughing nervously. "I never would have believed it was that horrific although I knew it was bad. To have the courage to bring that information to us after her debates with us about how slavery wasn't that bad took a lot of guts. Only Perry Mason would have had the tenacity to handle that report the way she did."

"I know. I never thought I would have to admit she did a better job at explaining the life of a slave woman than I could have," Tina said.

Shirley added, "She must have gotten those goods from a black sister. As racist as her ass is, I know she didn't come up with that knowledge on her own."

"Right, Shirley!" Tina responded. "She didn't come to class for a week. Someone had to have given her facts that profound. She even held me spellbound!"

Dawn smiled seeing May Bee's face and knowing she would have been pleased with her recounting of her life.

"Shirley, I wanted to say so badly, 'now I have respect for you, white girl.' At least you researched and gave a report without covering up and diluting the truth."

Dawn wanted to get up and tell them all she had witnessed but she knew the true extent of its horrors would be beyond their understanding. Shirley and Tina lived freer than they could ever imagine because of those female slaves who never lived at all. Females who simply existed in misery until death ended their lives. Dawn knew she had to have lived that kind of history to understand and tell about it. The descendants of those slave females will never understand the extent of the cruelties faced by their female ancestors. Her descendants, she also knew, would not want the memory of that time to dirty the image they have of themselves now.

"I'll tell you, Shirley, I acquired a new respect for that white girl. It took a lot of courage to get up there and report those facts when she knew no one was expecting it."

"Tina, what the hell was she thinking? She should know white people don't want that *shit* known. She will be ostracized by her white friends."

Dawn heard Shirley say, "It must have taken some powerful convincing to change that privileged, racist mind of hers."

"Wonder who the hell took on that job?" Tina asked. "She was talking like a woman who had been filled with the Holy Ghost."

Their laughter rolled over the partition. Dawn had to smile.

"Using black women's bodies in that way was a crime against humanity. We would have been better off if they'd lost both damn wars, Tina. Those Northern bastards turned our ancestors over to those white Southerners once they got what they wanted out of the war. Left them to be slaughtered after they fought to help the North win the war. Those freed slaves didn't know they would fall victim to Jim Crow Laws and the hangings, drownings and other killings that will forever shame this country. Except for the Native people living in this country, we all came here as outsiders. One coming of their own desire for a better life; the other forced over to work free all their lives. It sucks, doesn't it?"

Dawn closed her eyes seeing flashbacks of the cotton fields where the slave was thrown into the ditch still alive.

She wished for Meow at that moment.

"I can feel yer thoughts, Dawn." The sound of water splashing let Dawn know that Meow was somewhere close by. *"Dose sisters knows jus a litle of de American history ya now understan. Wonder what thay thoughts would be if thay saw and felt what ya saw and felt firsthand?"*

"I don't know Meow. I have little doubt that they would have been as shocked as I was."

Dawn no longer heard their conversation as the scene in the cotton field reappeared in her mind. A gray mist in the air choked her. She held her breath. Seeing statues swaying in the hot sun. The scene disappeared as she continued to listen to their conversation.

Shirley said, "They are always telling us we need to return to Africa. Where in Africa? We don't really know where on the continent of Africa those Africans took us from."

"No, we really don't," she listened to Tina say. "Especially if it was deep in the jungle where the white slave traders couldn't get to. And like the white girl once asked, what did they get for selling us? Whatever it was, they sure as hell don't have it now, not that I can see. Plus, we have no understanding of the different African cultures any more than European or the English culture is understood by white Americans whose ancestors have lived in America as long

171

as ours have. This country belongs to us the same as it does them. Talking about it's our *first* every time we do something that they believe only white people should be able to do. That's bullshit. The Native people in this country are the only firsts, everyone else is second." Laughter filtered through the partition once more.

"Believe me, girlfriend," Shirley huffed, "the only African Americans in this country are immigrants allowed in here after we insisted if they were letting white immigrants come in, they had to let black immigrants in from African countries as well. Those Africans brought with them their culture that shaped the people they are. Yet, white people now want to act as though we are immigrants the same as they are. Seems to me they are giving them favor over us when their ancestors never worked free a day in this country."

Dawn thought to herself, *they only know what they were told or read. What if they had lived their lives the same as May Bee who found a way to love even in the hell she lived? What they are saying is true, but these women have little understanding of why they are so bitter. The history they learned was written by men who had neglected to include the full extent of the shame of what the female slave endured.*

172

What she had experienced was horrific but even that was speculative. Meow had already informed her she hadn't seen the worst. She thought it such a pity that her white ancestors were foolish enough to think their genes only changed the color of the people they enslaved. Dawn knew, though she hated the thought of it, that descendants of slaves were people who had learned to live the same as white people lived; believing the same fairy tales white people believed. Now that she had begun to understand history better, she saw that even their behaviors were the same. Nothing about black Americans made Dawn think of the Africans who came to America from Africa after the 19th century.

"We are just white people in drag," she heard Tina say. More laughter filtered through the partition as Dawn listened to the shuffling of papers.

"I'm simply a female American who needs to get to her class," Shirley said. "Nothing we do is different from them, even the way we treat each other. We use color as our standard for importance, placing more value on light skin within our own race especially by our men when it comes to their women."

"What we haven't realized is that even education is a way to keep us separated from each other; as if we're better than others of our race who couldn't acquire an education. We are not." Tina added. "I'm afraid it's just as Tony says, we are all brainwashed."

"Tina, you would have to go there, wouldn't you? Well like I said, I believe in karma and karma will get their asses. They got payback coming. But you know what, Tina?"

"No, what?"

"The next time I see Dawn I am going to say hello, maybe sit down and chat with the white girl."

"You know something, Shirley."

"No, what?"

"Karma and white people are friends, otherwise it would have done them in a long time ago. It's only you and me that karma comes to. And about me speaking to that white woman, I don't know. White women have that privileged brain that always gets in the way when they approach black women, talking about we're intimidating like they're not. But after today, I think I will give the white woman her respect and address her favorably as well. She deserves at least a hello. Who knows, she might know something about my history even I don't know. After *that* report from those privileged lips everything is up in the air.

Let's get out of here before we miss our next class and end up in the air," Tina said as Dawn heard feet walking away.

The vision she saw on the plantation again consumed her thoughts. There was another class she should attend but she knew she must go back and find out what happened to May Bee and her babies.

As Dawn gathered her own books, she looked up to see Tony looking down at her. Before she could stand, he took a seat across from her with his long legs extended beyond the table. She looked at him wondering what they had to talk about that had not already been shouted out in class.

"Where, may I ask, did you find so thorough a document like the one we were privileged to hear?" he asked with a glare that turned into a smile.

"From May Bee, it all came from May Bee."

"Who in the hell, may I ask, is May Bee?"

"She's a friend of mine. She has a Ph.D in American History as well as Literature."

"I'm surprised you accepted her findings as facts. She, of course, must be a sister. I can't see a white woman coming up with a document so devastatingly thorough and be willing to acknowledge those facts. Especially sharing them with another white woman."

175

Dawn did not like how that sounded. When the facts were presented, she accepted what came from that discovery. She stared at him puzzled by his statement. "What is that statement you just made supposed to mean?"

He looked down at his hands, "I should have challenged you to a report on the male slave's history."

Dawn gazed beyond him to see the blistered body of the male slave tossed in the ditch. She couldn't get over Mindy's quiet announcement that her sister had a blind male slave hung because she thought he looked at her disrespectfully. All those slave men at the mating party used to create free labor.

"Nope," Dawn said. "The female slave gave me enough to report on. Too much brutality creates findings too bizarre for the brain to receive."

"Those findings you reported were bizarre."

"What do you mean?" she listened to him sigh.

"How the slave woman's life had been in detail. What a machine. More than twenty-two million slaves she produced in free labor for this country. What a woman. A study could be done on her reproduction cycle alone."

"According to my research, she had the most bizarre existence of any woman in this country," Dawn replied.

"I think many things that have happened in this country have approached the bizarre."

"Like what?" Dawn asked.

"When my mother was a little girl, she told me they were not allowed to attend white schools in Georgia, so they built their own beautiful school. The white people waited until night, covered themselves in white sheets and burned it down. Doesn't that seem bizarre to you?"

"Too bizarre!"

"They thought white people would be pleased since they wanted them in separate schools and told them they needed to learn proper English—especially how to *pronounce* words correctly."

His statement took Dawn back to May Bee's language learned within the horrible c*lamor of chains.*

"Not that it got us treated any better. In fact, it caused us more harm than good. Your people never respected our efforts to prove we were good enough to be a part of the human race no matter how much we mimicked you. Even with Jackie Robinson and Jessie Owens, you always sought ways to put us, or I should say keep us, in our place. A place always beneath you."

Dawn's mind wandered back to the slave woman who had to wear that red wool scarf only because she wanted it known that she was not a thief. Proving that even during slavery, the people enslaved wanted to be respected. Dawn remembered her skin to be as light as Tony's. The fathers who threw their sperm to the wind got slapped in the face with the DNA they passed down through generations. She couldn't believe not one medical doctor informed them that part of them lived in those babies they were producing.

She closed her eyes as the big blue catfish smiled at her. Winking its left eye, its southern voice rang in her ears. *"What does it matter Dawn when it's all American history?"*

"What does it matter Tony?" Dawn said mimicking Meow. "It's all American history." She smiled at him thinking, it's her history the same as it's his history because they were both Americans with ancestors born in this country farther back than the Revolutionary War.

"I've never understood why my people wanted us to mimic you whites. My mother and father, her mother and father down through generations, told us we had to get an education so that we could prove we were as good if not better than white people. They never realized that white peoples never wanted us to prove ourselves to be better or even as good as them. In fact, the more we proved we were your equals, the more determined you were to prove we were not. Something you feared we would become." They eyed each other.

"Every illness that came along, it was always us who drew more cases than any white person, according to you. No matter how many of us acquired college degrees it was always the poorest of our race you gave statistics on; all of our shortcomings you made us aware of. We could prove nothing to you because in your minds all you could see was our black skin— skin you hated. Those of us wearing our britches below our asses were getting as much if not more attention than any black man in a suit. It is sad my people could never see it."

"Tony no matter what was thought of your people you are here because they survived to overcome those cruelties. That is what I hoped to have conveyed. I discovered that many of their actions came from lack of knowledge or not getting the true understanding of the knowledge they had at that time." Dawn thought of the conversation she had just listened to between Shirley and Tina and what the black female students now thought of her. "I am the same person I was a week ago. I simply have information that has changed my understanding of the history I once believed was true."

"Where is God when you need Him? He's right on time every time, Dawn because even though you believe you are the same, that report you gave tells me you have changed in how you see your country's history."

"It's both our country's history, Tony; yours as well as mine. Color has nothing to do with a country's history. It's what happens in that country that determines its history and since what happened in this country is about your ancestors and mine. It's both our country's history. There is no such thing as black history or white history or even native history after the sixteenth century. It became American history; one people one nation. It's all of ours no matter how screwed up it is." Dawn rose. "I have another class to attend." She left him seated there in full thought of their conversation.

CHAPTER TWELVE
DAWN TALKS WITH HER FATHER

At dinner that evening her mother asked.

"How was your report received?"

"Astounding, according to my instructor. The students seemed to have accepted my findings, even the African American students thought it was on point, Mom. The best. Can you believe it?"

The smiles on her parents' faces indicated they were pleased. She continued to pick at the food on her plate.

"Dear, you don't seem as happy as you should be," her father said as both her parents stared at her.

Dawn looked at them wishing she could feel happy. Her thoughts went back to that last night. May Bee pleaded with her not to forget her and to let her classmates know of the miseries the female slave was forced to endure. Dawn realized in the world of slavery no kindness was given the slave or was it simply an illusion and white people were the ones who would really be played in the end.

181

What could her parents tell her when they didn't even know they needed to reexamine their own views of history and how it played out in their favor? She knew they lived indifferent to all but their own comfort. They'd been taught to play the role in the continuation of the superior race syndrome. She needed to know where was God when you needed Him? Dawn abandoned her poorly eaten dinner and headed to her room.

Later, Dawn looked up from her computer as her father took a seat next to her.

"What has you troubled, dear?"

It would be like him to sense something was bothering her. She hesitated. How should she explain her new awareness? Dawn loved her parents and hated bringing up uncomfortable topics to either of them. She'd never had a conversation with her parents about this aspect of American history.

"We're a strong race of able-bodied people. Why? Tell me why dad, did we have to lower our principles to feast on the lives of others?"

Her tears stained her cheeks and spoke of her sadness. She believed her father would not understand how she felt.

"We didn't need to drag those Africans over in chains to work free for us when we could have built a great nation without slave labor."

All she could see in her mind's eye was that hot blistering sun burning the life out of those forced to work in it with nothing except dirty drops of water to hydrate their bodies. Not to mention the lives of the female slaves used as machines to produce babies so that free labor could continue to build this nation.

"Tell me, dad, why did we become vultures stealing lives to work free for us?"

She saw the sadness in his eyes.

"Dawn I'm afraid slavery brought with it a sickness that changed us into horrible shameful human beings. In fact, it brought out the worst in us as a race of people."

Dawn stared at her father realizing he understood.

"You must have discovered this in your research."

She nodded her head *yes*.

"I know many say that slavery was always around even in biblical times, but modern man should have long ago evolved beyond the savagery that took place in modern slavery."

Dawn felt her father's arm around her. She was learning insight from him much like the odd professor.

"We did nothing except brutally destroy their humanity and shame ourselves."

"Why didn't you tell me? All this time growing up I believed, like my friends, that other races of people came to exploit the wealth we earned by the sweat of our own labor. I had no knowledge that our history was cursed with acts that today would send a man to death row." Dawn bit into her lips as she thought of her own past beliefs about slavery.

A frown formed on her father's face as he spoke. "It did worse than that I am afraid."

She looked at him with concern.

"We soon became nefarious people once slavery was introduced to our nation. Things we never believed one should do to another human being soon became a way of life for us."

Her father moved closer giving her his full attention as she continued to share her concerns. "Dad, our ancestors who used the female slaves' bodies for sex didn't realize they were reproducing part of themselves."

Tears spilled from Dawn's eyes as she remembered the mating party and those painful splinters that had to be pulled out of May Bee's behind because of the wooden animal trough she was forced to lay in.

"Our ancestors did that while working them in hot-ass fields until they were the living dead! Explain that to me, Dad."

Dawn stared at her father wanting to share with him her haunting memories of slave life.

"If we were so superior why did we use inferior people to help us build this country?"

"Because we saw them as inferior."

"They were seen as *inferior* because we took them away from their land, language and culture. We chained and shackled them then used them to fight both the Revolutionary and the Civil War. After all they did, we then turned our backs on them. Our promises meant nothing."

Dawn looked into her dad's eyes for answers.

"Honey, over seven hundred thousand Americans died in that horrible war if you count the people no one bothered to remember."

Dawn watched her father finger the watch on his arm.

"It was a war we now glorify with sedated memories. A war that was fought over human lives and the need to control this country." He sighed then said, "After Lincoln's assassination, those poor souls became problems we wanted to rid ourselves of, so we gave them back to the people who

185

had enslaved them in the first place. It's a shame how we pretended they were free."

"People who had fought side by side with Union soldiers. What honor was there in that, Dad? I don't understand it, especially after we had fought our own Revolutionary War."

"Everything we did back then now slaps us with a history we are ashamed to remember. Why do you think it was a subject I never discussed with you?" Her father rubbed his chin again as if in deep thought. "I'm afraid our history will live with us until this civilization ends. I wonder if the next one will learn from our mistakes?"

"Let's hope they don't learn the same as we learned from the civilization before ours," Dawn said.

"What is that?" he asked after a deep sigh.

"Absolutely nothing to be proud of. One day the questions I'm asking will be asked by every white child who learns to think with his or her own brain. The only power I have over an ant is the heel of my foot. My choice is whether I will remove my heel, or destroy it simply because I can."

"I love you. You know that don't you?"

"I know, father that you love me enough to shelter me from the truth. If I had never done that report I would have lived my life in ignorance? I will always love you, but I will always be sad for our shameful American history."

CHAPTER THIRTEEN
DAWN GOES BACK

The next Sunday Dawn drove down to where she hoped Meow would be. She ran to the gate and pulled the red handle to lift the latch.

"Meow come get me. I must go back and find out what happened to May Bee and her babies." She looked up and down the river. *Where is God when you need Him? I must know.* "Come, Meow. Let's go find them. I don't care if I never get back. I must know what happened to them."

"Well if dat's de case come on, honey chile, let's git out 'f hare 'for I git locked inside agin." Meow flopped on the bank, opened his mouth. Before she knew it, Dawn found herself back on the river bank, She looked for May Bee but nothing looked the same.

"What happened to May Bee and her babies?" Dawn asked looking at the catfish sticking halfway out of the water. It blinked its huge lime eyes and yawned but said nothing.

"Today is Sunday, Meow. May Bee and her babies should be here."

Meow laid there with its eyes closed as if it had gone to sleep.

"Do you believe in karma?" she asked.

The catfish ducked under the water splashing its tail. With just his lips out of the water he spoke, "*Even Meow don't mess wit karma. Ya never know when it's comin' or how. It can embrace ya wit a kiss or take yer life under. I can't be out of de water in dis dry air more dan a few minutes so it will be up to ya to find yer way back. If ya don't see May Bee come on back. I'll wait for ya right hare.*" The catfish disappeared underwater.

Dawn turned searching for the path back to the plantation. It seemed simple enough, but everything looked different now. As Dawn walked through what was once a wooded area, there were now no trees to speak of just wild gray brush. The heat from the sun was dry and arid. Breathing was difficult. The atmosphere looked dull and cloudy. As she walked into the clearing where slaves burned to death picking cotton in the cotton fields, Dawn stared in shock at the scene before her. It was the scene she had witnessed in her visions. Thousands of bodies stood planted in the ground just like the cotton that had once stood there. None of the faces had eyes and they all swayed in unison.

"Where is May Bee?" she cried aloud as she walked towards the bodies planted in the sandy dirt.

"Where is May Bee?" Dawn heard vibrating through the hot air.

Somehow, she understood the telepathic communication of the planted beings.

"What is that sound? It comes from a distant time." One of the beings communicated. "What year is this? What are you? Why are you rooted in the ground like plants?"

Dawn felt no fear of these strange things as she walked closer to see that the plants were human but not in the same sense that she was.

"This is the year 2416."

Though there were no mouths on their faces she understood them.

"What year is yours?" they asked her.

"I'm from the year 2016." *How did I get this far into the future?* Dawn started to worry now. *Oh no, Meow was supposed to take me back in time, not ahead!*

"You are from a primitive time," a being communicated.

Dawn stared at the weird looking beings swaying back and forth.

"We developed our genes to become superior to any other humans on earth. As the superiors of all of mankind, we magnified and perfected our DNA in ways no other race could duplicate; or so we thought. We then exterminated all others."

"How do you reproduce yourselves?"

"We developed the scientific processes to duplicate ourselves without the primitive method of reproduction. In this way, we could eliminate the production of genetically inferior or defected offspring. Mating, as you know it, was too inferior for our superior minds."

"How do you eat?" Dawn asked seeing no mouths.

"We consume nutrients without the need to ingest them from the outside. Our organs function two hundred years before our bodies disintegrate."

Dawn looked at the broken bones that lay on the dusty earth. She wondered if those bones belonged to one of them.

"With our superior reproduction systems in place, new forms developed regularly. Our communication is superior as well. Our thoughts are transmitted one to another eliminating primitive communication methods such as audible language.

"How do you move about?" Dawn asked growing mortified by the stump people swaying in the hot sun.

"Before *they* came, we could go anywhere and do anything we conceived of. You must become one of us and help us defeat *them*. We can then live again with no inferior beings to shackle our superiority."

Who had come? Dawn wondered. *Where was she? What were these* things? W*hy did they need her?* Dawn touched the blonde hair of one of the beings that reached to the ground. It was cold and hard; she flinched in horror. The plantation had vanished. There was not one slave. The plantation house, the cotton, the slave shacks, all gone.

"What are you doing here? What happened to the slaves living on this plantation?"

"This is the new world. The term slave has not been used since the old world ended."

"What happened to the old world? What happened to all the people? All of you look white."

"There are no white people – only *us* and *them*."

"Forgive me, but I don't understand what you mean. You are white. Everyone I see is white."

The planted humans never stopped swaying.

"Our ancestors believed we were the master race and there was no need for any other race. As our technological superiority advanced so did our definition of the human race. We were the only *humans* on this planet until they came. Their intelligence was more superior than ours and there was not enough of us to fight *them* off. They placed us in tubes and easily changed the molecular structure of our DNA to meet their needs. Planted in the ground. We became their food source!"

Before Dawn could ask another question, a sudden loud roaring filled the air. The robot-like forms stopped swaying. No one spoke or acknowledged the other. All communication halted and they stood as statues.

Dawn looked skyward horrified at the giant, white-haired beasts towering over the human plants; their gray garb blew in the thick, dusty air.

Dawn stood transfixed with horror as each beast grabbed and consumed its fill of the planted humans. Blood ran like a river and its mist sprayed through the air. The sound of crushing bones was deafening as bodies were torn from the gray dirt and swallowed whole by the hideous super-beings. Dawn choked and vomited from the debris that filled the air.

They somehow sensed her unfamiliar DNA and she was grabbed up and taken to an area where life forms floated inside glass tubes soaking in strange green oil in preparation for *planting*. Dawn knew she, too, would soon be soaking in the green oil. She cried out for Meow, but there was no splashing—that big old catfish couldn't save her this time.

"Where is God when you need Him?" she cried out in desperation.

Just as a mechanical arm tilted her body toward the tubes of green oil, May Bee appeared out of nowhere.

"Not her! She will come with me," May Bee commanded reaching for Dawn's hand.

They began to move backward in time as Dawn's head spun with visions of people and places.

Soon she and May Bee stood in the wooded area that Dawn remembered in 1842. It was the path that would lead her back to Meow and her own century.

"Ya go now dat catfish be awaitin."

"May Bee, where are you? What happened to your babies?"

"Me and my babies in heben, chile. De game is don' pass fo' us now de game is come fo' yer kind."

"May Bee, what game are you talking about? What happened?"

May Bee smiled as she shook her head. "Wit jus a little love and kindness like ya brung, we all coulda been down thare happy but thare was none in de hearts of them dat owned us. If de game is lost agin maybe May Bee and hur babies see ya in heben."

Dawn stood with tears in her eyes. May Bee no longer wore a rag around her natural hair and the simple brown dress she wore fit her petite body. Her face glowed with youth and a smile replaced the worn weary look of a slave.

"May Bee, where is God when you need Him?"

"Chile, God is ever whare when ya need Him to be. I'm hare ain't I? May Bee say she won't 'llow no harm to come to ya. Ya safe now. Go on. Find dat catfish."

Dawn's heart filled with sadness as May Bee disappeared into thin air. Remembering what she just escaped, the fear of being caught again by those creatures from the future overwhelmed her. Dawn sprinted back the way she had been told. When she got to the river's edge, she called out to Meow. The brown water splashed.

Even with water all over her, Dawn's tears were visible.

"For a minute there I thought you would become a part of the future. I took the wrong turn. Sent May Bee to

save you. By the year 2416, I will have moved back into your world many times to play the game of life."

Dawn thought while staring at him. *Who was this fish? His voice no longer sounded the same.*

"Meow, I don't like that game. No one expects it. It's too horrible!"

She could hear its voice but couldn't see the catfish. A white cloud appeared in the sky.

"It's not the game of life that's horrible, Dawn. The rules remain the same, but few ever learn the game. Each civilization has its own game coming. No man sees it coming until the evening has darkened the day. It is the wise ones who know how the game of life is to be played to win. One must learn the rules of the game. When you study your human history, you will find there's only a few that have won the game. Few ever learned to play by the rules. The slave masters never realized it was not the slave they owned but life itself. To control life wisdom must be applied."

"Where is God when you need Him?" Dawn asked.

"Don't you know by now? God is life and life is everywhere. It's those who control life without using wisdom that bring me back to play the game again and again."

The big blue catfish now appeared as the hairy figure in the sky she had seen with May Bee and the other slaves.

"You played the game and won. May Bee and her babies won because you were willing to learn the rules and understand how to win the game. It will be up to you to teach the rules to those who don't understand the game of life. A game that is played in every civilization."

The space traveler known as Meow moved upward beyond the clouds. Dawn watched its wide fishtail wave through the air and disappear as her hands rested on the red handle of the Corps of Engineers underground marine life gate.

God had been there all the time allowing her to see what she needed to see. All of it in the realm of the unexpected.

Meow.

Other books by the author: "Looking for Trouble" published under Meow The Louisiana Catfish, The Ms. Anna Trilogy; "Ms. Anna and The Tears from The Healing Tree", "The Two Worlds of Ms. Anna", "Ms. Anna The Promise Keeper", Published under Helen Collier

We are always seeking to discover other planets and their life sources. Who knows, perhaps there are space travelers who move throughout our world, hidden from us, who have discovered how the game of life should be played.
If so, what can they teach us before the evening has darkened our day?

Meow.

Made in the USA
Middletown, DE
15 September 2019